Three to Kill

Jean-Patrick Manchette

Translated from the French
by Donald Nicholson-Smith

CITY LIGHTS BOOKS
SAN FRANCISCO

Original text © 1976 by Éditions Gallimard
This translation © 2002 by Donald Nicholson-Smith

All rights reserved.
10 9 8 7 6 5 4 3 2 1

Cover design and photo: Stefan Gutermuth
Book design and typography: Small World Productions
Editor: James Brook

This work, published as part of the program of aid for
publication, received support from the French Ministry of
Foreign Affairs and the Cultural Service of the French Embassy
in the United States. Cet ouvrage publié dans le cadre du
programme d'aide à la publication bénéficie du soutien du
Ministère des Affaires Etrangères et du Service Culturel de
l'Ambassade de France représenté aux Etats-Unis.

Ourvrage publié avec l'aide du ministère français chargé de la
culture—Centre national du livre.

          Library of Congress Cataloging-in-Publication Data
      Manchette, Jean-Patrick, 1942-
[Petit bleu de la côte ouest. English]
Three to kill / by Jean-Patrick Manchette ; translated by Donald
Nicholson-Smith.
          p. cm.
      ISBN 0-87286-395-6
      I. Title: 3 to kill. II. Nicholson-Smith, Donald. III. Title.
      PQ2673.A452 P4713 2002
      843'.914—dc21

                                              2001042123

CITY LIGHTS BOOKS are edited by Lawrence Ferlinghetti and
Nancy J. Peters and published at the City Lights Bookstore, 261
Columbus Avenue, San Francisco, CA 94133. Visit us on the
Web at www.citylights.com.

1

And sometimes what used to happen was what is happening now: Georges Gerfaut is driving on Paris's outer ring road. He has entered at the Porte d'Ivry. It is two-thirty or maybe three-fifteen in the morning. A section of the inner ring road is closed for cleaning, and on the rest of the inner ring road traffic is almost nonexistent. On the outer ring road there are perhaps two or three or at the most four vehicles per kilometer. Some are trucks, many of them very slow moving. The other vehicles are private cars, all traveling at high speed, well above the legal limit. This is also true of Georges Gerfaut. He has had five glasses of Four Roses bourbon. And about three hours ago he took two capsules of a powerful barbiturate. The combined effect on him has not been drowsiness but a tense euphoria that threatens at any moment to change into anger or else into a kind of vaguely Chekhovian and essentially bitter melancholy, not a very valiant or interesting feeling. Georges Gerfaut is doing 145 kilometers per hour.

Georges Gerfaut is a man under forty. His car is a steel-gray Mercedes. The leather upholstery is mahogany brown, matching all the fittings of the vehicle's interior. As for Georges Gerfaut's interior, it is somber and confused; a clutch of left-wing ideas may just be discerned. On the car's dashboard, below the instrument panel, is a mat metal plate with Georges's name, address, and blood group engraved upon it, along with a piss-poor depiction of Saint Christopher. Via two speakers, one beneath the dashboard, the other on the back-window deck, a tape player is quietly diffusing West Coast–style jazz: Gerry Mulligan, Jimmy Giuffre, Bud Shank, Chico Hamilton. I know, for instance, that at one point it is Rube Bloom and Ted

Koehler's "Truckin'" that is playing, as recorded by the Bob Brookmeyer Quintet.

The reason why Georges is barreling along the outer ring road, with diminished reflexes, listening to this particular music, must be sought first and foremost in the position occupied by Georges in the social relations of production. The fact that Georges has killed at least two men in the course of the last year is not germane. What is happening now used to happen from time to time in the past.

Alonso Emerich y Emerich had also killed people, a good many more people than Georges Gerfaut. There is no common measure between Georges and Alonso. Alonso was born in the nineteen-twenties in the Dominican Republic. His repetitious Germanic family name tells us, just like that of his friend and close comrade-in-arms General Elías Wessin y Wessin, that his family belonged to the island's white elite and sought to signal it in this way, to underline the purity of their blood, their complete innocence of any intermixing with inferior races, Indian, Jewish, black, or other.

In the last days of his life, Alonso was a fiftyish man with a dark complexion, a middle-age spread, and hair dyed at the temples, living on a large farm on a vast property at Vilneuil, a hamlet thirty kilometers from Magny-en-Vexin in France. In the last days of his life, Alonso went by the name of "Taylor." What little mail he received was addressed to Mr. (or occasionally Colonel) Taylor. The neighbors and the local merchants he had any dealings with took him for a North American or maybe a Britisher who had spent years in the colonies and made his pile in import-export.

Alonso was indeed very rich, but his existence was wretched. He lived completely alone. Nobody worked the land on his vast estate, and there was no domestic help, for Alonso wanted none. The only people he let in the house during the brief period he spent there, which constituted the last days of his life, were two guys with limited albeit precise word power who wore dark suits and came and went, in an indiscreet and out-of-character way, aboard a bright red Lancia Beta 1800 sedan. One of the two was smaller and younger than the other, with wavy dark hair and very pretty blue eyes. Women were attracted to him. After a while they would discover that the only thing he wanted from women was to be beaten. He did not beat them in return and had absolutely no wish to penetrate them. So women would break off with him, except for the perversely sadistic ones. But he got rid of the perversely sadistic ones the moment he realized they were getting pleasure from beating him. They disgusted him, he said.

The other guy was in his forties. He had a protruding lower jaw, a big mouthful of teeth, and desiccated hair with vivid white streaks. A scar traversed his throat in a wide arc, quite impressive. He had developed the habit of lowering his chin onto his chest to conceal it. He was tall and gangly, and this way of holding his head gave him a quite peculiar look. These two had also killed people, but there was no common measure between them and Georges Gerfaut. Nor were they at all like Alonso. For both, killing people was a second career. The younger had worked earlier in the hotel industry, first as a waiter, then as a trilingual receptionist. The other was a former soldier of fortune. Georges Gerfaut is a traveling salesman. His job is to sell expensive electrical equipment manufactured by his company, a subsidiary of ITT, to individual and institutional clients in various parts of France and Europe. He has a good knowledge of the devices he sells, for he is an engineer. As for Alonso, his trade was war. He was an officer in the Dominican army and a member of the SIM (Military Investigations Unit). The best years of his life were those from 1955 to 1960, spent at the San Isidro air base. He was not engaged in war at San Isidro. The only state with which the Dominican Republic can conveniently go to war is the republic of Haiti, because it happens to occupy the same island as the Dominican Republic.

All other countries are separated from the Dominican Republic by at the very least a large stretch of water. But in those years there was no war even with Haiti. Alonso was very comfortable with this. At the San Isidro air base, in concert with his colleague and buddy Elías Wessin y Wessin (the base commander and a man destined to play a slightly historical if ever so mediocre role), he would send planes of the Dominican air force as far as Puerto Rico, whence they returned bearing liquor and other goods thus liberated from the burden of import duty. Alonso and Elías lived like kings. And they were untouchable. For while Santo Domingo, in contrast to many other places, was untouched by war with any foreign power, here as everywhere social war was a fact of life. And here as everywhere the chief function of the armed forces was to prevail in the social war whenever the need arose. In this connection, the intelligence-gathering role of the SIM was essential. To San Isidro were regularly brought persons suspected of collusion with the class enemy, and the job of the SIM under Alonso's direction was to make them talk by beating them, raping them, slicing them up, electrocuting them, castrating them, drowning them in places ingeniously designed for the purpose, and cutting their heads off.

On 30 May 1961, Trujillo the Benefactor of the Fatherland got himself riddled with bullets on a road by a commando group whose members, along with some accomplices, were later apprehended. For Alonso and Elías the halcyon days were over, or almost. The sons of the Benefactor held on for 180 days; subsequently, under Balaguer's presidency, Alonso and Elías got the chance to prepare for the 1962 elections by massacring peasants in Palma Sola and eliminating the loyalist General Rodríguez Reyes. After the small-time democrat Juan Bosch was elected, Elías ousted him in favor of Donald Reid Cabral, Santo Domingo representative of the CIA—and of Austin cars. Less than two years later, Elías saw clearly that the democratic ex-cop Caamano would bring a revolution in his wake, and he had a wild old time unleashing his tanks, Mustangs, and Meteors, which were deployed notably in Santo Domingo's northern suburbs. These were the most dangerous areas, with their workers' militias and other swine plundering (*horresco referens*) the great Pepsi-Cola plant near the cemetery for bottles with which to make Molotov cocktails. The Americans, however, who just like Elías had perceived the real danger behind Caamano's moderate and so to speak Kennedyesque pronouncements, and consequently furnished Elías with overwhelmingly decisive support in terms of logistics, arms, munitions, helicopters, aircraft carriers, marines, an air bridge (1,539 flights), and a lousy stinking "neutral" corridor—the Americans, once victory was assured, promptly ditched Elías and exiled him to Miami. Tough.

Alonso, for his part, had been out of it since 1962. Alonso did not share Elías's thirst for power, merely his love of luxury. He had overseen the departure of the Benefactor's family, complete with corpse, national archives, and a truly amazing amount of money. This task had given him ideas. As the 1962 elections brought Juan Bosch to power, Alonso flew off to exile and to the vast pile of dough that he had sent on ahead.

It is possible that Alonso's mind deteriorated over the next few years—years for him of ever-more-hasty house moving. Or perhaps, after all, he had been a near-dimwit from the outset. It is well to bear in mind that even at the pinnacle of his power he was nothing more than a high-ranking military policeman, for this makes it less startling to contemplate him in the last years of his life, terrorized, admitting no one to his house, no gardener or household help, lest it be an agent of the CIA, of the Dominican government, or of some group of exiled Dominican revolutionaries. Truth to tell, Alonso was getting old. By the time he settled in France, not far from Magny-en-Vexin, he was a broken man. Broken enough, at any rate, to decide that he would not move again. Let us remember, too, that here was someone who, faced by the widow of an executed man refusing to believe her husband was dead, sent her the man's head through the mail, with a little something stuffed in its mouth. One would have to say that, even if Alonso's specific fears were unjustified, their basis was rational enough.

Not even the postman was allowed in: what scarce mail arrived had to be delivered to a box at the edge of the road, outside the barred entrance to the property. And, just in case the mail carrier might be tempted to overstep this rule, as indeed for any comparable eventuality, Alonso kept a dog trained for fighting, a bullmastiff bitch.

The land around the residence thus lay fallow, producing nothing, while the interior of the house, in the absence of any staff to look after things, fell likewise into disrepair. The locals grumbled to see the land going to waste and several times contemplated a protest. No doubt they would eventually have mounted one had not Alonso's death settled the question.

Until that moment, in the last days of his life, Alonso generally gave up trying to sleep at about five or six o'clock in the morning. He would leave his disordered bed and his upstairs bedroom. In the large kitchen, he would assemble a full-scale English breakfast for himself: fruit juice, cereal with milk, and a plate of fried food accompanied by strong tea; he finished off with rounds of toast that he cut in half on the slant and then spread with a thin layer of butter and a film of honey or marmalade.

After his breakfast, Alonso would pull on a tracksuit and run for a long time with short little strides across his property, across his land overrun by wild growth, in company with the bullmastiff bitch, whose name was Elizabeth. Then he went back indoors and did not budge for the rest of the day, save in response to a ring of the bell by a delivery person. In that event, he would first observe the barred entrance gate from a ground-floor window through very powerful binoculars. Once satisfied, he would leave the house and go down to the gate armed with a .38 caliber Colt officer's target pistol and take the delivery. He never allowed the delivery person onto the property and would carry provisions up to the house himself. Sometimes the said provisions were heavy—cases of whisky, for example—and Alonso would sweat profusely, and uncontrollable trembling would seize his calves or the side of his mouth.

In the living room of the residence was a West German stereo system manufactured by Sharp. This Alonso dusted fastidiously, even though the rest of the house's furniture and fittings were almost never cleaned and were now irrevocably covered by a layer of grease and grime. Alonso likewise dusted the quadraphonic speakers set up pretty much throughout the house, so that recordings could be heard everywhere, even in the two toilets and the two bathrooms. His tastes in music were very different from those of Georges Gerfaut. His LP collection fell into three categories. First, high classical: Bach, Mozart, Beethoven. Second, syrupy American popular singers: Mel Tormé or Billy May. Alonso never played anything from these two categories, however. What he played, from the moment he returned from his walk with Elizabeth, was Tchaikovsky, Mendelssohn, or Liszt.

As he listened to this music, Alonso would be sitting in his study on the ground floor; his land, so thoroughly overgrown, would be spread out behind his ever-closed windows; his Colt officer's target pistol would be lying on the corner of his work desk; and he would be writing his memoirs with a Parker fountain pen on sheets of onionskin. He wrote *very* slowly. Sometimes he failed to complete so much as a page in ten or fifteen hours of work.

He ate no lunch. Every evening around six-thirty he dined on canned food and fruit in the kitchen. Then he put the dirty dishes in a dishwasher already containing those left from breakfast. Alonso would go on working for a couple of more hours, then turn off the music, start the dishwasher, go upstairs with a book, and lie down on his still unmade and rumpled bed. He would wait for sleep to come, but oftentimes it did not. He would hear the dishwasher below going through the phases of its cycle, pausing and clicking. He would read indiscriminately in English, Spanish, or French—for the most part, the memoirs of military men or statesmen: Liddell Hart, Winston Churchill, Charles de Gaulle; or else war novels, especially C.S. Forester. He also had a stack of back numbers of *Playboy.* Now and again he masturbated without much success. Several times each night he got up and wandered through the house, book in hand, middle finger keeping his place, and his limp member as often as not dangling from his pajama fly. He would check to see that all the windows were properly closed. They always were. And he would give Elizabeth an extra helping of food.

Georges Gerfaut also killed Elizabeth.

3

Georges Gerfaut was traveling on Route Nationale 19 in his
Mercedes. He had just passed Vendeuvre and was approaching
Troyes in the middle of the night, his two speakers serving up
John Lewis, Gerry Mulligan, and Shorty Rogers. To left and
right a wall of shadows fled past at 130 kilometers per hour.
Then the Citroën DS overtook him.

It had given scant forewarning: a last-moment flash of its
headlights, then the Citroën zipped passed the Mercedes on a
blind curve, wobbled slightly as it swung back into the lane,
and vanished round the next bend in less time than it took
Gerfaut to say what an asshole.

Ten minutes passed before he saw the car again. In the mean-
time, nothing had happened, except that he had passed an old
Peugeot van with inadequate lights and been passed by a little
bright red sports car, probably Italian. That was all. But now
suddenly his beams picked up something at the edge of the
darkness. At the same time, Gerfaut saw stationary taillights on
the road up ahead; he eased up on the gas; the taillights began
to move and were soon literally swallowed up by the night (or
perhaps they had never been stationary in the first place and
some trick of the darkness had fooled him). The Citroën, in any
case, was not only stationary but off the road, one fender in the
ditch, the other all twisted and misshapen and rammed up
against a tree trunk. A torn-off door, hurled ten or twelve meters
farther along, lay half on the roadway, half on the grass, its window shattered. All this Gerfaut took in at a glance, as the
Mercedes, still doing eighty, cruised past the wreckage. He was
tempted to speed up. What held him back was less a sense of the
proprieties, or some categorical imperative, than the idea that

the people in the Citroën were no doubt there in the darkness noting his plate number and liable to report him for failing to come to the aid of a person or persons in danger. Gerfaut braked, not quickly, indeed with a distinct lack of conviction, and pulled up eighty or a hundred meters farther on.

Up ahead a pair of taillights—the Italian sports car? was it perhaps a Lancia Beta?—had just been enveloped by the night. Gerfaut looked about nervously, could see nothing behind but blackness. The Citroën, too, had vanished. Still gripped by the desire to continue on his way, he groaned between his teeth, shifted into reverse and backed up, zigzagging slightly, to the scene of the accident.

He pulled over onto the shoulder between two trees, along-side the detached car door. From the cassette player came "Two Degrees East, Three Degrees West." Gerfaut turned it off. He was possibly about to discover horribly mutilated corpses, a little girl with braids sticky with blood or people holding their guts in with both hands. Not the sort of thing you did to a musical accompaniment. He got out of the Mercedes with his waterproof electric flashlight and pointed it directly toward the Citroën. To his relief, he saw only a man, and he was standing up. A small man, with frizzy blond hair, the first signs of bald-ness, a sharp nose, and round glasses with plastic frames. The right lens was clearly cracked. The man was wearing a reefer and rough brown corduroy pants. He looked at Gerfaut with big frightened eyes. He was leaning against the hood of the Citroën and panting.

"Hey, there," said Gerfaut. "How are you doing? Are you hurt?"

The man moved vaguely, perhaps nodding, then almost fell. Gerfaut approached anxiously. His gaze fell by chance on a damp, dark area on the man's side that was just becoming discernible against the dark wool of his jacket.

"You're bleeding from your side." Gerfaut's mind spontaneously produced the odor of blood and its taste, and he thought, my God, I'm going to throw up.

"Hospital," said the man, and his lips continued to move, but he managed to add nothing more.

It was the man's left side that was bleeding. Gerfaut grasped his right arm, wrapped it around his own neck, and tried to hold up the injured man as he led him over to the Mercedes. A car of indeterminate make screeched by at high speed.

"Can you walk?"

The injured man made no reply, but he walked. Drops of sweat gathered below his receding hairline and on his upper lip where short whiskers grew.

"S'pose they come back?" the man mumbled.

"What? What's that?"

But the man would not or could not speak anymore. They reached the Mercedes. Gerfaut helped the injured man lean against the car and opened the right rear door. Grasping the backrest, the man hauled himself slowly onto the seat, where he lay on his back.

"Shit! Shit! I'm bleeding," he said with a mixture of regret and rancor. He spoke like a working-class Parisian.

"You'll be okay. You'll be okay."

Gerfaut pushed the injured man's legs in farther, slammed the back door, and climbed briskly into the driver's seat. He was thinking that the blood would soil the leather upholstery; or perhaps he was thinking nothing. The Mercedes started up. During the journey Gerfaut said very little, and the injured man said nothing at all.

They were at Troyes in less than ten minutes. It was twelve-twenty. There was not a cop to be seen. Gerfaut hailed a tardy passerby, who directed him to the hospital. The passerby was drunk, and the directions were confusing. Gerfaut almost missed the way, losing time. In the back, with great difficulty but without audible complaint, the injured man had removed his jacket. Beneath it he wore a black polo-neck pullover. He had folded his jacket in four and was pressing it to his side to stanch the bleeding. Just as they arrived at the hospital, he passed out. Gerfaut parked hurriedly at the entrance to Emergency. He leaped from the car and entered an ill-lit lobby.

"A stretcher! A stretcher, quickly!" he shouted and returned to the car to open the rear doors.

Nobody came out of the hospital. To the right of the lobby Gerfaut found a large glassed-in reception area with two girls in white blouses behind a counter and four other people: an Algerian and an old couple sitting on tubular-metal-and-plastic chairs and a guy in his thirties with a white complexion and flaccid cheeks, in a suit but no tie, leaning against the wall and biting his nails.

"Come on! For Christ's sake!" yelled Gerfaut.

Two male nurses appeared in the lobby with a gurney.

"We're coming!"

Efficiently, they lifted the injured man out of the car, laid him on the gurney, and left at top speed through the lobby. Before they disappeared, one of the nurses turned to Gerfaut, who was hesitantly following in their wake.

"You need to register him, okay?"

Gerfaut was by now standing some four or five meters inside the lobby, close to the side door leading to the reception area. The aged couple and the Algerian had not budged. The tieless thirty-year-old man had stepped up to the counter. He had a form in front of him and a ballpoint in his hand, and he was talking animatedly with one of the girls in blouses.

"I don't know her," he was saying. "I found her lying on my doormat. I could see that she'd been taking something; I couldn't leave her like that; I brought her here in my car, yes, but I don't know who she is, I don't know her, I don't even know her name. I can't help it if she decided to commit suicide on my doorstep, can I?"

Sweat was running down his pale forehead.

Gerfaut got out a Gitane filter and slowly retraced his steps, trying his best to appear inconspicuous, his gaze directed vaguely toward the floor. He need not have bothered: no one was paying him the slightest attention. Once outside, he got back in his car and drove off in a hurry.

A moment or two later, a medical resident and a bareheaded policeman burst agitatedly into the reception area and loudly demanded to know where the person was who had brought in the man with gunshot wounds.

4

"It's stupid. You must be mad," said Béa.

Béa was Béatrice Gerfaut, née Changarnier, by background Catholic on one side and Protestant on the other, Bordelaise on one side and Alsatian on the other, bourgeois on one side and bourgeois on the other; by profession a freelance press agent, formerly a teacher of audiovisual techniques at the University of Paris at Vincennes and, before that, manager of a health-food store in Sèvres—a superb and horrible mare of a woman: big-boned and elegant; with big green eyes; thick, healthy, long black hair; big, hard white breasts; wide, round white shoulders; a big, hard creamy ass; a big, hard white belly; and long, muscular thighs. At this moment, Béa stood in the middle of the living room wearing sea-green silk day pajamas with flappy elbow-length sleeves, feet bare on the plum-colored carpet beneath the immense flares of the pants. She began to pace up and down the room, trailing wisps of Jicky perfume behind her.

"You mean you left just like that, without a word to anyone? You didn't give your name? You don't know the guy's name? You didn't even say where you found him? Do you have any idea what you're telling me?"

"I don't know what it was," said Gerfaut. "All of a sudden I was sick of it. Everything was just pissing me off. It's a feeling I get now and then."

He was sitting on a leather-and-canvas sofa with decorative strapping. He had been there for just a few minutes. He had taken off his jacket and tie and undone his shoelaces. In pants and shirt, his collar open and his shoes loose, he sank back into the couch, a glass of Cutty Sark loaded with ice cubes and drowned in Perrier precariously balanced on his left knee, a

Gitane filter in the corner of his mouth, and sweat stains at each armpit. Vaguely perplexed, he had an urge to laugh.

"Sick of it?" protested Béa. "Pissed off?"

"Look, I just wanted to get out of there."

"What a dope!"

"That," said Gerfaut, "is quite beside the point."

"Absolutely not. What must they have thought? You show up with a car-accident victim and then you run off. Tell me this, what are they supposed to think?!"

"He could explain it himself. Anyway, screw it."

"What if he didn't know what happened to him? What if he was in shock? Or dead?"

"Stop shouting—you'll wake the kids up." It was past four in the morning.

"I'm not shouting!"

"All right, but you don't have to be so damn rude."

"You mean assertive."

"No, I mean rude!"

"Look who's shouting now!"

Gerfaut picked up his glass and forced himself to drain it slowly without taking a breath, his Gitane filter clasped upright between thumb and right index finger, filter downward on account of a long cylinder of ash that was threatening to fall on the floor, there being no ashtray to hand.

"Listen," he said, when he had finished the drink, "we'll think it all over tomorrow. I haven't killed anybody, I did what I had to do, and more than likely we'll never hear any more about it."

"For God's sake!"

"Béa, please. Tomorrow, okay?"

His wife seemed about to explode. Or, possibly, to burst out laughing—for, despite appearances, Béa was not what you would call a nag or a ball buster: as a rule she was outgoing and self-assured. After a moment, she turned away in silence and disappeared into the kitchen. The ash of Gerfaut's Gitane fell onto the carpet. He got up and stamped on it, rubbing, spreading, erasing its traces with his shoe, then went over to the Sanyo stereo and began very quietly playing Shelley Manne with Conte Candoli and Bill Russo. Recrossing the room, he crushed his cigarette out in an alabaster ashtray, which he took back with him to the sofa, then he sat down again and lit another Gitane filter with his Criquet lighter. The quadraphonic speakers softly dispensed soft music. Gerfaut smoked and contemplated the living room, only a portion of whose lighting, the dimmest, was on at present. An elegant penumbra consequently enveloped the armchairs and matching sofa; the coffee table; the off-white plastic cubes bearing a cigarette box, a scarlet plastic lamp in the form of a mushroom, and recent issues of *L'Express, Le Nouvel Observateur, Le Monde, Playboy* (American edition), *L'Écho des Savanes,* and other periodicals; the record cabinets containing four or five thousand francs' worth of classical, opera, and West Coast jazz LPs; and the built-in teak bookshelves with several hundred volumes representing the finest writing ever produced by humanity and a fair amount of junk.

Béa returned from the kitchen with two Cutty Sarks and a tender ironic smile. She sat down next to her husband, handed him one of the glasses, and tucked her bare feet under her. She rolled a strand of hair around her index finger.

"Okay, then," she said, "let's not talk about it; we'll see later. How was your trip, otherwise? Did it go well? Did things pan out?"

Gerfaut nodded with satisfaction and offered a few details about a successfully concluded deal and about how he stood to collect a 15,000 franc commission over and above his monthly salary, which was about half that. He began to tell how at lunch the wife of the local rep had become horribly drunk and what happened then. But soon he seemed no longer to find it so amusing and abruptly ended his narrative.

"What about you?" he asked his wife. "How did you get on?"

"Oh, same old. The last two screenings of the Feldman are for tomorrow. Karmitz will distribute the thing for us, it turns out. Phew! You stink of sweat!"

"Well," said Gerfaut, "that's all I am, isn't it? A stink of sweat!"

"Oh, shut up!" Pushing herself up with her feet, Béa arched her back and stretched, showing off to advantage her fine build and the harmony of its simultaneously hard and soft embodiment. "Be quiet and finish your scotch. Take a shower. Then come and make love to me."

Gerfaut was quiet, finished his scotch, took a shower, and went and made love to her. In the doing, though, he banged his shoulder on the frame of the bathroom door, slipped, and almost fell and broke his neck in the bathtub as he was showering, twice dropped his toothbrush in the washbasin, and nearly destroyed his Habit Rouge deodorant atomizer. There were no two ways about it: either he was drunk from two drinks, or else.... Or else what?

5

The attempt on Gerfaut's life did not take place immediately, but it was not long coming: just three days.

The day after his late-night return home, Gerfaut awoke at noon. The little girls were at school and, being semiboarders, would not be home till evening. Béa had gone out about ten, leaving a message on the pillow. She could sleep for just four or five hours and still be fresh and energetic all day long. She could also on occasion sleep for thirty hours straight in a deep, childlike slumber. The message read: *9:45 a.m. Tea in thermos – cold roast in fridge – have settled up with Maria – back in afternoon (to pack) but second screening Antégor 6 p.m. si te gusta and if you can – LOVE.* (The last word was in English. The ink was purple and the handwriting was elegantly careless; Béa had used a felt-tip marker.)

Gerfaut went into the living room, where he found the thermos of tea on the coffee table along with zwiebacks, butter, and the mail. He drank some tea and ate two buttered zwiebacks and opened the mail. There were several subscription offers for business magazines and a few financial newsletters; a friend Gerfaut had not heard from in two years wrote from Australia that his married life had become intolerable and asked whether Gerfaut thought he should get a divorce; and on a green card Gerfaut's chess partner had indicated his fortnightly move. Gerfaut noted the move in his notebook, thinking that he wouldn't have the time to think about it right away, seeing that they were getting ready to leave on vacation, but then he replied mechanically, castling just as Harston had castled against Larsen when in the same position at the Las Palmas tournament of 1974. On the part of the green card left for correspondence, he wrote what was to be his address for the whole of the next month in Saint-Georges-de-Didonne.

Around two in the afternoon, shaved, showered, combed, deodorized, dressed, Gerfaut looked at himself in the hall mirror. He had a handsome pale oval face, blond hair, a forceful nose and chin; but he also had liquid blue eyes, and his gaze was slightly abstracted, slightly soft, a tad owlish and evasive. He was on the short side. Last summer, in clogs with gigantic heels, Béa had stood a few centimeters taller. His proportions, the breadth of his shoulders, his musculature were satisfactory, but no more than that; the exercises he did every day, or almost, had had some effect. Not too much of a belly for the moment, though there was danger there. The body in question was at present encased in Mariner briefs, a slate-gray jersey-wool suit over a white-and-slate striped shirt with a solid-white collar and a plum-colored tie; cotton socks; and plum-colored English shoes with much visible stitching (what is perhaps called overstitching).

The elevator bore Gerfaut straight down to his Mercedes in the building's underground garage. He started up, drove out into the street, wound his way to the Gare d'Austerlitz, and crossed the Seine. From the cassette player came Tal Farlow. In about twenty minutes Gerfaut reached the headquarters of his company, a subsidiary of ITT located just off the Boulevard des Italiens. He parked the Mercedes in the company's underground garage. The elevator took him first to the ground floor, where he slipped the green card, restamped and readdressed to his chess partner, a retired mathematics teacher in Bordeaux, into a mailbox. The ground-floor lobby was full of oraculating working stiffs. Gerfaut got back in the elevator and went up to the second floor. The second-floor reception area was also full of oraculating workers. A potted plant gently toppled over as Gerfaut struggled out of the elevator. A union representative from the General Confederation of Labor (CGT) stood athwart the stairs leading to the third floor. He wore a checkered shirt and royal-blue canvas pants.

"Excuse me, please," muttered Gerfaut as he pushed past.

"If Monsieur Charançon is afraid to come out," the union delegate was shouting, "we'll drag his fat ass out ourselves."

A bellow of approval went up from those in possession of the lobby. Gerfaut extricated himself from the melee and went down a corridor with Gerflex vinyl flooring. He reached his door and went in. In the anteroom Mademoiselle Truong was painting her nails scarlet.

"How do you manage?" asked Gerfaut. "With nails like that, I mean, you type a lot. Don't you break them?"

"It happens. Good morning, monsieur. Did you have a good trip?"

"Excellent, thanks." Gerfaut made for his office.

"Roland Desroziers is in there," warned Mademoiselle Truong. "Well, I wasn't going to fight with him, was I?"

"No one expects you to fight," answered Gerfaut, going into his office and closing the door behind him. "Hi there, Roland."

"Hi there, you little cop-out," said Desroziers, who was an ecological militant and a union delegate of the French Confederation of Labor (CFDT) and wore a black sweater and jeans; Gerfaut had been a militant with him in the early sixties in a radical fraction of the Seine-Banlieue Federation of the Unified Socialist Party (PSU). "It's talk, talk, talk in there," said Desroziers, "I came in here to get a drink." He had indeed purloined Gerfaut's Cutty Sark and was quaffing a large measure of it in a paper cup. "You don't mind me drinking your scotch, I hope?"

"Of course not," answered Gerfaut, smiling but peeking at the bottle and the paper cup to see just how much Desroziers had helped himself to. "It may be talk, talk, talk," he observed, "but that Stalinist bureaucrat says they're going to drag the boss's fat ass out of here themselves—those are his exact words—so you're going to be trampled underfoot if you sit around here drinking the rich man's booze."

"Shit!" said Desroziers, hurriedly sticking his nose back into the paper cup and slurping the rest of his drink. Coughing, he set the cup down. "I'm out of here!"

"Go ahead, set the place on fire, trash the computer, string Charançon up, why don't you," suggested Gerfaut in a dispirited tone as he sat down at his desk and reached for the whisky bottle to put it away. "All power to the workers' councils!" he added bitterly. But the CFDT man was already gone.

That afternoon Gerfaut took care of business pending, dealt with salespeople needing directives, and conducted a long discussion with his immediate subordinate, who would be standing in for him during July, and who, truth to tell, hoped through a combination of intrigue, servility, and betrayal soon to replace him completely and definitively. Gerfaut was for his part called in to see Charançon, who had had the greatest difficulty disentangling himself from the proletarian agitation. Charançon's face was flushed, and he wore a tiny Lions Club de France badge on his lapel and Pierre Cardin suspenders beneath his gray suit. Behind him on the wall was a poster under glass with pretty painted pink flowers and the English words HOME SWEET HOME inscribed in large, pale, pink frilly letters. Superimposed on the flowers and the pink inscription was a text in small black characters whose author was Harold S. Geneen, president of ITT. It ran as follows: *In different locations around the world, almost anywhere on the globe, rather more than two hundred workdays each year are given over to executive meetings at different levels of our organization. It is during these meetings, be they in New York, Brussels, Hong Kong, or Buenos Aires, that decisions are taken based on logic, on a business logic that leads to choices that are almost inevitable, for the simple reason that we are in possession of almost all the basic elements needed to arrive at decisions. Just like our planning, our periodic meetings are designed to clarify the logic of things and expose that logic to the light of day, where its value and necessity will be apparent to all. This logic is immune to all state laws and regulations. It is a part of a natural process.* There was no way of telling whether the presence of this poster in Charançon's office testified to a discreet sense of humor or to a terminal state of alienation. Charançon congratulated Gerfaut on the success of his negotiations of the last two days, and it was agreed that his bonus would be credited to his bank account in the course of July. Charançon poured two glasses of Glenlivet.

"Thank you." Gerfaut took the glass Charançon held out to him.

"They are completely mad," said Charançon. "Do you remember May '68? They were still out on strike in the middle of July—but they had no idea what they wanted! Remember?"

"When they do find out what they want, it'll be time for you and me to get a real job. Or pack our bags." Gerfaut sipped his whisky. "What they wanted was the collapse of capitalism."

"You bet your sweet ass they did, my friend!" agreed Charançon distractedly.

Back in his office, tidying up, Gerfaut was subjected to the usual erotic provocations of Mademoiselle Truong. She was continually crossing the room, bending over as far as she could to reach things, ostentatiously removing specks of dust from her eye, or standing on tiptoe, thighs and buttocks and breasts and arms all straining upward, to straighten the Air France calendar or the work schedule or one of the glass-mounted prints. At the same time, Gerfaut felt certain, had he grabbed her ass she would have screamed, made a scandal, or scratched her aggressor's cheek with those vicious-looking scarlet nails.... Gerfaut sent her out for *France-Soir* (Béa always made sure to pick up the more serious *Le Monde*).

The paper's suggested lottery numbers were three, seven, and twelve. Tanks and air power had been deployed against six thousand rebellious Bolivian peasants. An Eskimo had been shot and killed while trying to divert a Boeing 747 to North Korea. A Breton trawler had gone missing with its eleven-man crew. A woman had celebrated her hundredth birthday and announced her intention of voting for the left. Extratrerrestrials had abducted a dog in full view of its master, a crossing guard in the department of Bas-Rhin. And, in emulation of a recent fad on America's West Coast, a couple had tried to fornicate in public on a French Mediterranean beach, only to be restrained and arrested by the local police. Gerfaut glanced at the funnies, then tossed the newspaper into the wastebasket.

"I'm leaving now," said Mademoiselle Truong.

"See you tomorrow, then."

"What do you mean, tomorrow?"

"Oh, yes, I'm sorry. Until the first of August, then. Have a nice vacation."

"You, too, Monsieur Gerfaut."

She left. Gerfaut left soon after. It was about seven—too late to join Béa at the screening of the Feldman film. Gerfaut didn't want to see it, anyway. He could easily have left the office a couple of hours earlier, but he had wanted to show that, even the day before leaving on vacation, he had worked hard, gone beyond the call of duty.

After forty-five minutes of very slow progress through blocked traffic, with Lee Konitz accompanied by Lennie Tristano on the cassette player, Gerfaut left the Mercedes in its slot in the underground parking garage of his building in the thirteenth arrondissement and went up to his apartment. The little girls were there watching the regional news. (They watched anything that appeared on a television screen; for them there was no significant difference between the regional news and, say, *The Saga of Anatahan*.) The girls' bags and Béa's were almost packed. Gerfaut showered, changed, and did his own packing with the feeling that he was forgetting everything important, and served the girls cold roast beef with Heinz salad dressing and Bulgarian-style yogurt. Then he sent them off to bed; they left the room, insulting him in a muted but earnest way.

Soon Béa arrived, in good humor. As the two of them sat in the kitchen eating cold roast beef with Heinz salad dressing, she told him that Maria had that morning begged for the key to their apartment while they were away. Supposedly, Maria had broken off with her Berber boyfriend, who was looking for her and meant to kill her. Wasn't he the one who wanted to put her to work on the street? asked Gerfaut. Wiping the corner of her mouth with a paper napkin, Béa replied that that had been a joke. Maria's real plan, according to Béa, was to get the run of their place so she could bring the guy over, clean out their liquor cabinet, and screw. But, all the same, protested Gerfaut, what if the guy really was stalking her, the poor kid? Poor kid, poor kid!—she was big enough to take care of herself! was Béa's last word on the subject.

After dinner they tossed their paper plates into the trash, washed the other dishes and left them on the drainer, finished the packing, brushed their teeth, got into bed, read a few pages, she of Edgar Morin's latest book, he of an old John D. MacDonald, and went to sleep. Gerfaut awoke shortly after two in the morning and fell prey at once to an inexplicable and terrifying insomnia. He went and took half a sleeping pill with a glass of milk. He fell asleep again with no difficulty about three. Early the next morning, they all got up and left for their vacation. Gerfaut having had the forethought to take off work as from the twenty-ninth of June, traffic was free-flowing. This, and the invention of superhighways, enabled them to reach their destination in under seven hours, including a stop for lunch and without speeding. And so, on the night of the twenty-ninth of June, the family slept at Saint-Georges-de-Didonne.

The next day was the day they tried to kill Georges Gerfaut.

6

At eleven-fifty on the night of the twenty-ninth of June, one of the men who on the following day would try to kill Georges Gerfaut sat in the Lancia Beta 1800 sedan, which was parked fifty meters from Gerfaut's apartment building. In the back of the car were two metal suitcases. The first contained clothes, toiletries, a science-fiction novel in Italian, three very pointed and well-honed butcher knives, a sharpening steel, a garrote made of three strands of piano wire with aluminum handles, a blackjack, a 1950 model Smith & Wesson .45 caliber revolver, and a Beretta 70T automatic with silencer. The second case contained clothes, toiletries, six meters of nylon cord, and a SIG P210-5 9mm automatic target pistol. In a canvas bag on the car floor were high-power binoculars and an over-and-under M6 like those used by the U.S. Air Force, with a folding butt, one barrel being .22 caliber, the other a .410 shotgun. There were munitions, too, of various kinds, in thick wooden boxes in the Lancia's trunk. Should such an arsenal be considered impressive or simply grotesque?

The man in the car was at the wheel, with his chin sunk into his chest, his back against the back of the driver's seat, and a monthly comic book propped against the wheel's leather cover. The comic was called *Strange,* and it recounted the adventures of Captain Marvel, the intrepid Daredevil, the Spider, and various other characters. The man was reading with great concentration, moving his lips. A succession of emotions registered on his face; he was identifying to the hilt.

After a moment, the other guy, the one with the wavy black hair and pretty blue eyes, emerged from Georges Gerfaut's building, walked back to the Lancia, and got in beside his companion. The latter put his *Strange* into the cubbyhole in his door and wrinkled his nose with curiosity.

"I smell fat."

"Cooking fat, yes," said the other. "The concierge was making fries. Georges Gerfaut has left on vacation for a month. I have the address. It's in Saint-Georges-de-Didonne; the department number is 17."

First, the hit men consulted the dark one's diary to see what department had the number 17, and found out that it was Charente-Maritime. Then they took down a small atlas of French main roads that was attached to the right sun visor with an elastic band, perused it, located Saint-Georges-de-Didonne, and mapped out their route.

"I drive fast," said the one with the white streaks in his hair. "We can be there by this evening."

"Well, fuck that! Shit, no!" replied the dark man bitterly. "Let him wait. First, we'll have a big meal. Then we'll do a little sightseeing. Come on, why shouldn't we?"

"Mister Taylor said fast, Carlo."

"Taylor? What's he got to say about it? He's got nothing to say about it. Anyway, he's cool, totally cool."

The nostrils of the man with the white streaks flared tautly.

"Carlo, you really do smell of greasy food."

"What a pain in the butt you are!" Carlo reached into the back and opened one of the metal cases, took out a toilet bag and produced a bottle of Gibbs aftershave. He poured lotion into his palm and dabbed himself with it about the cheeks and under the arms. Then he put his tackle away.

"If we don't have to hurry," said White Streaks, "we can stop at Le Lude. It's charming, Le Lude. It has a delightful castle."

"All right then, if you say so. Start the car, for Christ's sake! We can't sit here forever!"

7

At the sound of Gerfaut clattering about in the kitchen and swearing between clenched teeth, the little girls came downstairs. Gerfaut didn't bother to scold them, even though, as he saw it, it was still too early to get up.

The girls were dressed. Gerfaut dug out denim shorts and a Lacoste shirt, and all three left for the seafront. It was already hot. The beach was completely deserted. A wooden refreshment stand showed no sign of opening up. The Mercedes made a right, cruised by a motionless funfair and a cemetery, turned left, and finally parked in a side street near an antique shop that also dealt in detective stories, varnished seashells, and comic books translated from the Italian. Gerfaut and the girls found a café open and settled themselves on perforated plastic seats in red, yellow, and pastel blue. They drank bowls of gray café au lait speckled with stray coffee grounds and ate butter croissants from a nearby bakery. Then they headed back. A breeze had come up, sand whirled across the beachfront road, and the shrubs planted in wooden boxes waved back and forth like carnivorous plants. The milky coffee formed a resinous lump just below Gerfaut's sternum.

He left the car in the street outside their rental house. In the main room, with the blinds raised and windows open, Béa sat in an immense white robe dipping a zwieback in Special for Breakfast tea from Fortnum & Mason's. She removed a crumb from the corner of her mouth.

"Where've you been? What got into you? Did you go to look at the sea?"

"We had breakfast!" cried the girls, as they raced noisily out of the room and up the stairs.

Gerfaut sat down at the table.

"Do you like the house?" asked Béa.

"For God's sake," said Gerfaut, "why can't we go to a decent hotel? In North Africa, the Canaries, any damn place—"

"Stop it—stop swearing!" chided Béa.

"Just so long as daylight doesn't come into the room at half-past five in the morning, and dogs don't bark, and cocks don't crow, and you don't have to hear all those horrible noises. Tell me why we can't! We can afford a good hotel, so why not?"

"You know perfectly well why not! It's not worth talking about it. You're only trying to bring me down."

"I want to bring you down? God in heaven!"

"Yes, you'd love that. But I'm not going to let you, so it's no use talking. If you don't like it here, you can go back to Paris."

"If I don't like it here! Christ!" Gerfaut surveyed the mildewed leather couch, the likewise mildewed easy chairs, the two Henry-the-Second sideboards, the two massive dining tables with their carved legs, the ten chairs (two sideboards, two dining tables, ten chairs—Christ!), and the door to the toilet, opening directly into the main room, adorned by the picture of a small boy in short pants, socks about his ankles, with blond curls, mischievous bright eyes, and rosy cheeks, turning his head cutely toward the viewer as he pisses against a Montmartre-type gas lamp.

Misreading Gerfaut's pensiveness, Béa thought he had calmed down and rested her head on his forearm. She told him he was tired from the journey and that he had slept badly and that she understood. Granted, the house was hideous—but they hadn't come to the seaside to stay indoors all the time. Anyway, they would rearrange things, take down the awful picture, consign one of the tables to the attic—"Christ alive," grumbled Gerfaut, "do you realize how much those things weigh?"—and the bedrooms weren't too bad, and the garden was just fine.

"Every year," said Gerfaut, "I think it's worse than the year before. Even if it's not."

"Every year," retorted Béa, "you decide that we'll never set foot here again, then you refuse to look at any houses. And when the time comes, we decide together at the very last minute that it wasn't really so bad last year. But we never have enough time off to come up here, so my mother has to choose—not that there's any choice left."

"This year, I'm sure there was some choice." Gerfaut got up from his chair and started mumbling about inflation and deflation and recovery and unemployment and how people were set in their ways and always went away in August, just for the month, so he was quite sure they could have had their pick for July.

"Listen," said Béa, "what's done is done."

"Your mother's an idiot."

"My mother's an idiot, yes," agreed Béa with disarming equanimity, "and we are having lunch at her house, and you'll do me the favor of having a shave and being polite."

Gerfaut burst out laughing. He dropped back into his seat and laughed theatrically, first throwing his head back, then shaking it and slapping his thighs. Béa calmly finished her zwieback. Gerfaut stopped laughing and wiped his eyes.

"One of these days," he said, "I'll suddenly go mad and you won't even notice."

"If there's any difference, I'll notice."

"Very funny," said Gerfaut sadly. "Very funny, I must say. What a wit!"

He went to wash and shave. When he tried to hang his hand towel on the rail, the thing parted from the wall with a grating sound and fell to the floor, accompanied by a small quantity of plaster and two bent screws. Gerfaut left the towel, the rail, and the plaster where they lay and drove to the co-op to shop for essentials. He returned with a good supply of breakfast cereal, oil, cheese, milk, spirits, wine, and mineral water, both still and sparkling. The little girls were lobbying loudly for a television set to be rented.

"You can't get a decent signal here," asserted Gerfaut.

"We did last year!"

"You need an outside antenna."

The girls scooted out of the house, overturning a chair as they went. They returned shouting that there was an antenna on the roof. Gerfaut surrendered and promised to take care of it.

"When? When?" the girls wanted to know.

"This afternoon, okay? I'll go into Royan."

They quieted down instantly as though some button had been pressed. Later, they all went on foot to Béa's mother's for lunch.

"You have to go to Royan for a television," the girls reminded Gerfaut when they came out of the old witch's house.

So Gerfaut took the Mercedes and went to rent a television in Royan. On the return trip he overtook a Lancia Beta 1800 sedan. Back at the house, whose hideousness he still couldn't hack, he plugged the set in. Finally, he undressed, slipped into an ugly green swimsuit, and left to join Béa and the girls at the beach.

It was five o'clock. The sun was leaden but baking hot. Inflation and deflation and all the rest notwithstanding, and despite the fact that it was only the thirtieth of June, there was a good number of people on the sand and in the water. Gerfaut wondered what it would be like in three days.

It took him easily five minutes to locate Béa and the girls. All three had already been in the water, sunbathed for thirty minutes, and covered up. Ensconced in a beach chair, wearing jeans and a crepe de chine blouse, Béa was reading Alexandra Kollontai. The girls, in T-shirts and overalls, were building a sandcastle. Gerfaut opened the other folding chair and sat next to Béa. The kids scampered up to make sure the TV had been installed and, once satisfied on this score, returned to their digging. Gerfaut stripped down to his trunks. The whiteness of his skin embarrassed him. He went in the water on his own.

A few minutes later, the two hit men got out of the Lancia, which was parked on the seafront. They both wore shorts. Neither of their bodies had a trace of fat. On the contrary, they were both very muscular, and muscular in the best way—harmoniously, with none of the excess of the bodybuilder. Each cast a brief admiring glance at the other's physique as they made their way toward the sea—and Gerfaut.

Gerfaut had entered the cold water without pleasure, advancing in stages as first his penis and balls, then his belly button, were immersed. At that point he had doubled up and plunged headlong into the drink. He was now swimming in slightly over a meter of ocean mixed with hydrocarbons, empty Gauloise packs, peach pits, orange peel, water from the Gironde River, and a trace amount of urine; all around him was a mass of little children, giggling teenage girls, beach-ball lobbers, spry old folks—there was even a black African in a bright red swimsuit. There were people at every point of the compass. In Gerfaut's ambit, the closest were at least three meters away and the most distant some twenty-five meters in any given direction. When the two hit men in shorts approached Gerfaut, he paid no attention. So he was much taken aback, as he touched bottom long enough to catch his breath, to be punched matter-of-factly in the solar plexus by the younger of the pair.

Gerfaut fell forward slowly; his mouth was open and the water rushed into it. The young assailant grasped his torso with both hands and held the middle of his body under the water. White Streaks grabbed Gerfaut's hair with his left hand and clamped the right on his throat, forcing his fingers into the flesh around the larynx and trying to strangle Gerfaut while simultaneously stopping him from getting his head out of the water.

As the first punch landed, Gerfaut's solar plexus had been just level with the surface. Since the blow had been delivered at a tangent to the water, its force had been mitigated. Consequently, Gerfaut's capacity to react was now not so compromised as it might otherwise have been.

Blindly, sensing the water running freely into his bronchial passages and his epiglottis quivering in the grasp of attacker number two, Gerfaut fumbled around in the filthy sea, brushed a pair of thighs, seized someone's nylon-clad genitals, and did his very best to tear them off.

His throat was released. He got his face above the water. He was struck on the top of the head and the temple and forced back under once more. He had barely been able to gasp a little air. He had been vouchsafed a brief water-streaked vision of the children, the giggling adolescent girls, the ball players, and the black African. An eruption of laughter, shouting, and ocean spray (and a guy braying hysterically—"Pass, Roger, pass!"). A whole tiny universe oblivious to the fact that Georges Gerfaut was being murdered! He deliberately directed his head downward instead of trying to come up for air as one might have expected. Wrenching his body from the grasp of the blue-eyed hit man, he performed an underwater somersault and resurfaced throwing up bile, and butted the younger assailant hard on the jaw. Someone delivered a hammer blow to his kidney. A single scarlet thread of a thought occupied Gerfaut's mind: gouge their eyes out and tear their balls off—kill these sons of bitches that are trying to destroy you!

And then, after a long-drawn-out minute, the two hit men decided to flee. Because they weren't finishing off their prey. Because their prey had turned into a kind of hysterical machine hurling masses of water around and threatening at any instant to scratch one of their eyes out. And because at any moment now Gerfaut would get enough air into his lungs to cry out, and the people around, who for the time being were peacefully playing their little games and minding their own business, would inevitably realize that something was amiss. Escaping would then entail fighting a way through a veritable throng while waist-high in water. The prospect did not fill the hit men with enthusiasm. So, for all these reasons, the pair decided to flee.

For a few seconds, Gerfaut continued thrashing about, groaning and moaning and unaware he was all alone. By the time he got his wind back and realized that he had really been released, his two attackers were already on dry land. It took Gerfaut a moment to spot them trotting back up the beach. A trickle of blood was visible on the small dark one's leg, and he was hobbling. Then they left the beach and crossed the road and were lost to Gerfaut's view. The beachfront road was elevated above the sand; there was a balustrade; and parking on the beach side of the street was forbidden. A minute or so later, Gerfaut saw a red sports car start up in a hurry and head off. He pointed vaguely, but he couldn't even be sure that it was the aggressors' car. His arm fell limply to his side. He cast a glance at the bathers around him.

"Murderers!" he yelled, but his cry lacked conviction.

The black African looked at him suspiciously, then swam off

with an impeccable crawl. The others carried on throwing themselves into the water, playing ball, cackling and yelping. Gerfaut shook his head and waded slowly back to the beach, doing breathing exercises. As he made for Béa and the girls, his legs felt distinctly wobbly and his throat was burning. He sat down in his deck chair.

"How was the water?" asked Béa without raising her eyes from her book.

"Tell me this," said Gerfaut abruptly in a hoarse voice. "Have you been pulling some kind of stupid practical joke on me?"

"What are you talking about?" Béa turned toward Gerfaut and pushed her sunglasses down onto the end of her nose. Over the frames, she contemplated her husband with wide eyes and not a little impatience. "What's that on your neck? It's all red."

"Nothing. It's nothing," replied Gerfaut in a tone that discouraged further inquiry.

Béa raised her eyebrows and plunged back into her Kollontai. Gerfaut whistled a few bars of "Moonlight in Vermont," broke off, and looked uncertainly at Béa. Twisting in his chair, he scanned the beach and the sidewalk of the beachfront, narrowing his eyes, but he could see nothing out of the ordinary. In point of fact, the two hit men were now four kilometers away in a café-restaurant. They were grumbling and bickering and had just ordered two dozen oysters and a bottle of Muscadet de Sèvre et Maine as consolation for their recent pitiful failure. Once again, Gerfaut shifted his position in his deck chair, leaning down to root in Béa's beach bag for a book by someone called Castoriadis that dealt with the historical experience of the workers' movement. For a while he pretended to read. A bit later, with the sun a little lower in the sky, Gerfaut, Béa, and the girls returned to their rented house to change and freshen up. Then they went out again and made their way to a Breton crêperie near the seafront between the amusement park and the bike-rental store. Béa hated cooking. They ate quickly because the girls wanted to be back in time for a film showing that evening on television. The movie was *Pickup on South Street,* directed by Samuel Fuller. Gerfaut could no longer stand the feelings he was having. About eight-twenty-five, he announced that he was going out for cigarettes. As night slowly approached, he wandered around Saint-Georges-de-Didonne. Gerfaut almost wished that the two men would reappear and attack him again—if only to put an end to his uncertainty. He found himself on the beachfront, and when a bus came by on its way to Royan, he caught it. Once in Royan he resumed his strolling. At ten o'clock, he boarded a train from Royan to Paris. Afterward, curiously, the only thing he recalled from his walk around Royan that evening was the sign in the window of a store called Fairy Fingers: LINGERIE—GENTLEMEN'S SHIRTS—HOSIERY—NO-TIONS—SPECIALISTS IN DELUXE UNDERGARMENTS—BABY WEAR—LACE—KNICK-KNACKS—BIBS—FINE HANDKERCHIEFS—BUTTONS—FORM-FAST AND REDUCING CORSETS (NEVER RIDE UP—NO NEED FOR GARTERS). ALSO ALL TYPES OF GIRDLES AND BRAS—PLEATING—OPENWORK EMBROIDERY FOR BED LINEN—BUTTONHOLES—STOCKING REPAIR—BUCKLES.

"Do you know what I remember?" cried Gerfaut, alarmingly jubilant. "The only thing I remember is the sign in a shopwindow! I know the whole thing by heart!" And he recited it word for word.

"Drink your coffee," counseled Liétard.

Gerfaut complied. He was sitting in the back room of Action-Photo, a small shop not far from the town hall of Issy-les-Moulineaux, where his old friend Liétard sold cameras, film, movie equipment, binoculars, telescopes, and a mass of smaller items. Liétard wore a red shirt and worn-out black pants. He had a long, thin intellectual's face and a gentle manner, but these traits were misleading. He is one of those who were in the entrance to the Charonne metro station at a bad moment: 17 October 1961, when police cornered Algerian protestors there. He is also one of those who came out alive. The next year, six months after his release from the hospital, Liétard set upon a lone policeman late one night in Rue Brancion, beat the man savagely with his own baton and left him naked, two ribs and jaw broken, handcuffed to the iron railings around the Vaugirard slaughterhouses.

"You must be wiped out," said Liétard. "Did you sleep on the train?"

"No, I didn't! Of course I didn't!"

"You can lie down upstairs if you like. You ought to, you know."

"I couldn't possibly sleep now."

"Would you like me to give you a sleeping pill?"

"It wouldn't work."

"Give it a try, anyway."

Gerfaut protested weakly. Liétard brought him two white tablets with a glass of water, and he took them.

"You must think I'm losing it."

"I don't think anything. I'm listening, that's all. I have to open up shop, okay? It's nine o'clock."

Gerfaut nodded distantly. Liétard got up from the table and went through into the front. He opened up and almost immediately had to serve a customer wanting a 36-exposure roll of Kodachrome X. By the time he returned to the back room, Gerfaut was already half asleep and half slumped over the corner of the table. Liétard helped him upstairs via an interior spiral staircase covered with riveted jute matting. Gerfaut undressed almost unaided and lay down on the bed. He promptly began to snore—or perhaps "buzz" would be a more accurate word. He half awoke once, vaguely noticed that it was daylight, wondered where he was, and fell back to sleep. When he came to, night was falling outside the shutters. Gerfaut got up and got dressed. Liétard appeared at the top of the spiral staircase with a cup of coffee in his hand. Gerfaut rushed at him and grabbed him, and coffee sloshed from the cup and filled the saucer.

"You bastard!" shouted Gerfaut. "Have you telephoned my wife?"

"No. Should I have?"

"Did you telephone the cops? Or anyone?"

Liétard shook his head in perplexity. Gerfaut let go of him and stepped back with a grimace of apology.

"Should I make us steak tartare?" asked Liétard. "For old times' sake? I've bought all the makings."

Gerfaut nodded.

"Do you think," asked Liétard, once they were seated before

plates of ground steak black from overspicing, "do you think they were trying to do away with you on account of that guy you picked up on the road the other night?"

"Me? But why?"

"Well, I mean, what you were saying last evening. How you thought they imagined you had run the guy over or something like that, and how they might be friends of his out for revenge."

"I'm sorry. I don't follow you," said Gerfaut, shaking his head vigorously.

Liétard repeated what he had said.

"Oh, well, yes. I suppose that could be."

"You ought to talk to the police." Liétard was pouring Médoc.

"I don't want to."

They looked at each other as they munched.

"You can stay here for a few days if you like," offered Liétard.

"No, no."

"Tomorrow afternoon, on the box—oh, what shits they are, though! Did you see the Fuller yesterday? They showed the dubbed version, the morons! But of course, you couldn't have seen it, could you? What was I saying? Oh, yes, tomorrow afternoon they are showing Edward Ludwig's *Wake of the Red Witch*. It's really wild. I always cry at the end. You know what knocks me out every time—and I don't know how this works, but it never fails—it's when characters that are dead come back to life at the end, like in *Yang Kwei Fei* or in *The Ghost and Mrs. Muir*. Even with *The Long Gray Line*—every time I think, shit, what militaristic trash, but then at the end—it always happens— when Donald Crisp and dear, old Maureen O'Hara show up again, wham!" Liétard used his fingers like a mime to suggest tears running down his face.

"Uh-huh," murmured Gerfaut, who hadn't the slightest idea what Liétard was talking about.

They finished their steak tartare and wine. It was late in the evening now. They lit cigarettes. Gerfaut asked Liétard if he had any music to play.

"Such as?"

"A little blues from the West Coast?"

"*Kleine Frauen,*" quoted Liétard, "*kleine Lieder, ach, man liebt und liebt sie wieder.*" And he translated: "'Little women, little songs, you love them and go on loving them.' A bit of blues from the West Coast? That's so typical of you! Sorry, old pal, all I have is hard bop."

"Even back in high school we were never on the same wavelength."

Then Liétard spoke a little about himself. The store brought in enough for him to survive. He had no plans to marry. The year before, he had had an affair with an American woman.

"I have written a film script," he said, "but I am not happy with the end. I have to get the end right. And I may write a book on the great American cameramen."

"Béa—my wife—works for the film industry as a press agent."

"That's great. We should get together. Not just on that account, of course. I mean, generally."

Before long, Liétard said that he would soon be going to bed, and Gerfaut said he would be leaving.

"Are you going back to Saint-Georges-de-Didonne?"

"I don't know. I suppose so."

"No point driving yourself crazy. It was probably just two nuts, guys who were drugged up, who went for you in the water for no particular reason. There are creeps everywhere, you know."

"Do you think you could let me have a gun?"

"Sure, if it would make you feel safer. But let's be quick about it."

The two men went rapidly back upstairs. Liétard opened a chest of drawers containing several cloth-wrapped boxes. After a moment's reflection he removed one from its dull blue covering and produced an automatic pistol engraved with the words BONIFACIO ECHEVARRÍA S.A.—EIBAR—ESPAÑA—"STAR."

"This one you can take with you. A guy left it here. He completely forgot about it—a funny story. Well, not so funny, really, if you think about it. A friend of a friend. He came from South America, but he was French. His father was tortured to death by the Nazis during the Resistance. He had been turned in—and the mother knew who by. The kid was raised in South America by this mother, who taught him to hate—you know, so that he would go and kill the man who had ratted on the father. Heavy stuff. Anyway, the lone avenger set out on his mission, but it turned out he was just fantasizing with his peashooter. Once he got here, he made no real attempt to find the informer—who, for all I know, may have been dead for years. He met a girl, they got married, and I think they are both teaching in Aix. The guy simply forgot his Mauser at my place. A 7.63mm."

"Thank you," said Gerfaut.

Liétard gave him a brief rundown on the operation of the weapon. The magazine was full, but the ammunition was ten or fifteen years old. Liétard had no more. The two men went down to the ground floor and bade each other farewell. Liétard half raised his metal shutters to let Gerfaut out, then lowered them once more. Gerfaut made his way to the Mairie d'Issy metro station. The Star was in his jacket pocket. Softly, he sang words to the effect that your youth is gone, and your lover too.

10

From Liétard's Gerfaut went straight home. After turning on the water and electricity, he went from room to room putting all the lights on. The place was comfortable and humdrum. It was impossible to imagine killers lying in wait in the broom closet. Gerfaut turned off most of the lights, took a shower, shaved, changed, and settled down in the living room with a Cutty Sark that was tepid because the refrigerator had not yet had time to kick in, there was no ice, and the weather was so warm. For a time he listened to Fred Katz and Woody Herman. At half past eleven he sent a telegram, via telephone, to Béa, telling her how sorry he was to have left without warning, impossible to contact her sooner, would explain later, letter to follow, everything all right. By this time, Gerfaut was into his sixth whisky, which no doubt explains why he promised a letter, even though he fully intended to return post haste to Saint-Georges-de-Didonne. What's more, he began to write said letter, and twice spilled whisky over his efforts.

"I plan to return to Saint-Georges very quickly," he wrote. "My little flight must seem quite incomprehensible to you. Quite frankly, I don't understand it very well myself. I'll explain everything. I suspect that nervous exhaustion is the main culprit. Struggling all the time—and for what?" Gerfaut crossed out this last sentence. "This year has been hard, and I've had to struggle a great deal. There are times when I want us to pack everything in and go and live in the mountains and grow vegetables and raise sheep. Don't worry, though—I know this is all idiotic." He closed his letter with declarations of love, having put away another four whiskies. By now he had ice cubes. He opened a fresh bottle of Cutty Sark, but there was no Perrier. He tore up the whisky-splattered missive and tossed the pieces into the kitchen trash can. Then he stretched out full length on the couch; he meant to take a fortifying nap, for just a few minutes, but instead he fell into a deep sleep.

The telegram to Béa reached the post office at Saint-Georges-de-Didonne at nine the next morning. The two hit men were parked in their Lancia on the corner of a small residential street, whence Carlo, through the windshield, could observe the Gerfauts' vacation home some two hundred and fifty meters away. Around nine-fifteen he saw Béa and the girls leave for the beach with a bag and towels. He grabbed a pair of binoculars from the passenger seat and focused them on the woman and the two kids. The glasses were very powerful, and Carlo could clearly see that Béa's features were drawn and that she had been crying recently.

"Hey, look at this! Psst! Hey!"

White Streaks sat up in the back where he had been dozing and locked one hand onto the back of the front seat. With the other, he rubbed an eye energetically. He yawned.

"I was dreaming of the old man."

"Taylor?"

"Taylor's not old. No, the other one. The old man the other day."

The other day, the two hit men had gone into the old man's office. First, they told him what was what. Then, as White Streaks held him, Carlo hit him repeatedly across the neck with the blackjack, effectively crushing his throat. Finally, the two threw the old man out of the window, and he crashed onto the pavement three stories below.

"The broad and the brats have just left for the beach," said Carlo. "He'll be out, too, any minute now."

"Carlo, I tell you I don't think he's in the house."

"Let's not have that discussion again, okay?"

"Last night there was only the wife and little girls in the main room, and no lights on anywhere else. So since he hasn't come back...."

"He must have been in the john," Carlo asserted—and he smirked as though he had said something funny.

White Streaks shook his head. He seemed about to argue the point, but he thought better of it.

"Here comes the mailman." he said.

Indeed, a telegraph messenger on a bicycle was just then braking in front of the Gerfauts' rental house. He leaped from his machine and in the same motion leaned it against the hedge, then he hurried into the garden and mounted the front steps with a martial air. He rang the bell. As though by magic a telegram had appeared in his hand. After a moment he rang again and then again. He hammered loudly on the door with his fist. Eventually, he slipped the telegram half under the door, returned to his bike, and pedaled off.

"He sleeps like a log, the asshole," said Carlo. "Perhaps we should just go in there and fix his wagon."

White Streaks was instantly halfway out of the car.

"Hey, no!" said Carlo. "I didn't really mean it. Don't screw up, Bastien."

But Bastien was already on his way to the house. Carlo started the Lancia up, but Bastien turned around, still walking, and motioned him to silence. Carlo cut the engine and let himself sink into the back of his seat with a sigh of exasperation. His back hurt; the two men had spent the night in the car.

Bastien reached the front of the house, pushed open the wooden gate into the garden, and went and retrieved the telegram, which he opened delicately. His lips moved silently as he read the message. Then he replaced the telegram under the front door and returned to the car.

"It's from him," he reported. "From Gerfaut. It's signed Georges and it's a telegram sent by telephone, sent by Georges Gerfaut from his address in Paris. He isn't here—he went home. So? Who was right?"

"Fuck you!"

"Come on. Who was right? Tell me who was right!"

"You were, dickhead."

Bastien got back in the car—in the front this time and at the wheel. He started up.

"Whoa!" said Carlo. "Where are we going?"

"Paris, you prick."

The Lancia revved into motion and vanished into the distance. A few moments later, one of the Gerfaut girls appeared and went into the house. She failed to notice the telegram. After a while she reemerged with a set of plastic balls for *pétanque* in an openwork plastic carrier. This time she spotted the wire. She picked it up, read it, and sped off toward the beach.

11

It was the telephone that woke Gerfaut. He sat up with a grunt, almost fell off the couch, and caught himself by grabbing the back of it with one hand as he rubbed his eyes with the other, clenched-fisted, rather as the hit man Bastien had done an hour and a half earlier. It took Gerfaut a moment to remember where he was. His eyes were crusted, his breath fetid, his tongue dry. He went toward the telephone, scratching through the opening of his shirt at the middle of his chest, where some men have a thicket of hair. He picked up the receiver. As he did so, he noticed with irritation that the stereo had been on all night. Someone shouted into his ear, and at first he didn't know who it was, then he realized it was Béa.

"Oh, wait a second, excuse me."

She shouted again. She was sobbing. She wanted an explanation. Gerfaut meanwhile was crossing the room, managing, not without difficulty, to carry the whole telephone with him. Reaching the stereo, he turned the power off, briefly felt the turntable, the tuner, and the amp (the two last were very hot to the touch), and winced.

"What happened was I had a fit of depression." He sat down on the couch and placed the phone on his lap while holding the receiver to his ear with his shoulder. He looked around for a cigarette. Béa was shouting over the line.

"Hello!" he shouted in his turn. "I hear you very badly." With his finger Gerfaut kept rotating the dial. Each time he did so communication was interrupted. "Hello? Hello?" he shouted. "Béa? I don't know whether you can hear me. Don't get worried. I love you. Just a bit of depression. I am coming back. Hello? I said I'm coming back. I'll be there this evening. Tomorrow at the latest. Hello?" He was still fooling with the dial, and everything he said reached Béa badly broken up. For her part she had the greatest trouble making herself understood.

Gerfaut ended the conversation abruptly by depressing the crossbar of the telephone with his index finger. Letting the bar back up, he listened for the dial tone, then replaced the receiver and put the telephone back in its usual place. Then he unplugged it altogether. Let Béa call back if she wanted to. She would hear unanswered rings; he would hear nothing at all, not even a ring.

He went through to the kitchen and made himself some tea. As it was brewing, he showered, shaved, and changed—and the two hit men kept rolling toward Paris in their bright red Lancia Beta 1800 sedan. Gerfaut drank his tea and swallowed spoonfuls of marmalade without any bread and read a few pages of an old issue of *Fiction* magazine. When he had finished, he plugged the telephone in once more and called a car-rental company and then a taxi service.

Around eleven o'clock, a cab dropped Gerfaut off at a garage, where he took possession of the Ford Taunus he had reserved. For a time he drove around Paris aimlessly. The two hit men were speeding along the highway. Carlo had taken the wheel. Bastien dozed to his right. They had quarreled for a moment when Bastien told Carlo the exact wording of the telegram. Carlo had maintained that it made most sense to wait in Saint-Georges for Gerfaut to return. But Bastien argued that the words "letter to follow" in the message indicated that Gerfaut was not coming back any time soon. They exchanged several volleys of "soft in the head" and "retard." In the end, Bastien had weakened. He sat up abruptly and swore.

"I dreamed of the old man again."

"Me, I never dream."

"Me, neither, not usually."

"Sometimes I wish I did."

"Sometimes," said Bastien, "I dream of castles, castles—how can I explain it to you? I dream of castles that are all gold, with towers and spires. I know—just like Mont-Saint-Michel, you know what I mean? But mountainous—the landscape all around is mountainous—and mists everywhere."

"What I'd like is to dream of women."

"No, no. Not me."

"That woman the other time," said Carlo. "I liked that."

The other time, after throwing the old man out of the window, they had gone to the woman's house. They made quite sure that she knew nothing. Absolutely sure. At one point, Carlo had forced the woman to beat him. She had not liked it. Nor had she liked the rest. Carlo had liked it a lot.

Generally speaking, even if you went back to the very beginning, to the Mouzon contract, you had to say that all their business dealings with Colonel Taylor had gone like clockwork. But then they had run into this moron Georges Gerfaut. A traveling salesman, though, is usually very easy to kill. Carlo and Bastien were well placed to draw comparisons because they had exercised their skills in the most varied social milieus. They were now beginning to get quite angry with Georges Gerfaut.

About one-thirty that afternoon, Gerfaut dug into frankfurters and fries in a café-restaurant. In theory, it was a fine clear day, but in practice you couldn't see very far on account of the air pollution. The women passing by wore scanty summer clothing. But as for everything else—the cars moving at a crawl through clouds of exhaust fumes and jazz from Radio FIP 514, the hollow eyes of the rushing people, the general din, the watery and adulterated taste of the sausages as Gerfaut bit into them—it was all shit. He would so much rather have been in a place where he could see things around him that were not in his own image, where everything did not speak to him of himself—in short, an inanimate landscape. He returned mechanically to his apartment, arriving about three-thirty. He tidied up, then played music very loud—the Joe Newman Octet with Al Cohn—as he tossed a few things into a small suitcase. Almost immediately, the doorbell started ringing repeatedly in a most authoritative way. Gerfaut ran to the couch, where he had left the jacket he had been wearing when he left Saint-Georges-de-Didonne. He took the Star from a pocket, released the safety, and cocked the weapon. He went to the door, unlocked it, and sprang back with the automatic behind his back and his finger on the trigger. After a moment, the concierge of the building pushed the door open and contemplated Gerfaut with concern: he had tripped, and he stood with legs crossed, balancing on his heels, one arm still behind his back and his other elbow against the wall for support.

"Oh, it's you, Monsieur Gerfaut," she said doubtfully. "Aren't you on vacation?"

"Huh?" Gerfaut backed into the living room. A few seconds later, the volume of the music was lowered considerably, and when Gerfaut returned he no longer had one hand behind his back.

"Weren't you supposed to be on vacation?"

"Yes, indeed. But I came back. I forgot something."

"You must excuse me. I was on the stairs and I heard music. I wondered who in heaven's name would be playing music at Monsieur and Madame Gerfaut's."

"You were right," said Gerfaut. "That was kind of you. In

fact, it's reassuring to know you keep such an eagle eye on things."

"We do what we can, but we are only human, you know. By the way, two gentlemen from your work came around asking for you."

"Two gentlemen," Gerfaut repeated noncommittally, careful not to sound curious.

"Well, I should say one gentleman. The other waited in their car. I hope I was right to give your address."

"My address," said Gerfaut in the same tone as before.

"At the seaside, I mean."

"Oh, yes, of course. A young dark fellow and a tall guy with white in his hair, was that it?"

"The young one, yes, definitely. The other...." The concierge indicated with a hand gesture that she had not been close enough to get a clear view of the second man.

Gerfaut was now leaning with his shoulder against the wall. He was staring vacantly at a point somewhere above the concierge's head and appeared to be musing, daydreaming. His silence and distractedness made the concierge uncomfortable.

"Oh, well, I'll have to be going. It's very nice talking to you, but I have lots of things to do."

For the last ten minutes, the Lancia had been standing on a pedestrian crossing just under a hundred meters from the building's entrance. A woman came out with an Airedale on a leash. The Airedale was sixty centimeters long and a male (unlike Alonso's bullmastiff, Elizabeth, who measured nearly seventy centimeters). The woman with the Airedale crossed the street in front of the building and got into a Datsun Cherry parked opposite. She started up the car and left. Carlo had his motor running the moment he saw the woman's right-hand

JEAN-PATRICK MANCHETTE **55**

blinker light up. The Datsun was barely out of its spot when he slid into it. Carlo was alone in the Lancia. Bastien was keeping watch from a café with a good view of the parking lot on the far side of the Gerfauts' building. The two hit men had begun by telephoning Gerfaut's apartment from the café. The phone had rung, but no one had picked up.

"You wait and see, shithead!" Carlo had said vehemently. "He's gone back to his wife."

All the same, Carlo was not very keen to drive the six or seven hundred kilometers all over again just to check this out.

The two agreed, therefore, that to start with they would simply wait and watch. See if Georges Gerfaut came home. If he didn't, when night fell they would break into his apartment to make absolutely sure.

And if he wasn't there, they would send a fake telegram to Saint-Georges informing the guy that there was a water leak and that he should call home as soon as possible. The two would then spend the night in the apartment. In the vacation period, Carlo and Bastien loved to spend nights in temporarily vacant apartments. Especially Bastien.

"It's like we're tourists," he would say. "People's apartments are like other countries."

"Oh, shut up, dickhead," Carlo would reply.

In short, if it turned out by the next morning that Gerfaut had indeed returned to Saint-Georges-de-Didonne, they would take stock—but they would no doubt go back there and kill him, most likely with a rifle.

"Because," declared Carlo emphatically, "I have had it up to here with half-measures."

"I'm just a bit depressed," Gerfaut was writing. "It will blow over. Please don't get upset. I plan to come back by a roundabout route—do a little touring, drive through the Massif Central." Once again he closed his letter with declarations of love. He promised to be in Saint-Georges "within three days, four at the most." He sealed the envelope, addressed it to Béa, and went down to mail the letter. Carlo was stunned to see him come out of the building. Gerfaut had the letter in his hand. He walked the fifty meters to a mailbox near the corner of the building and dropped the envelope in the slot. Then he returned to the entrance and went back in. Carlo started the car, drove around the building as quickly as he could, and stopped with a great screech of brakes in front of the café where Bastien was ensconced. Gerfaut took the elevator from the lobby to the basement, climbed into the rented Ford Taunus, and started the engine. Carlo was now making emphatic hand gestures directed at Bastien. The man with the white streaks in his hair placed five francs on the counter and rushed out of the bar. The bottle-green Ford Taunus, with Gerfaut at the wheel, exited the parking garage and merged into the traffic. Bastien got into the Lancia next to Carlo, and the two set about tailing the Taunus.

"He really pisses me off, this guy," said Carlo in disgust.

It was four-thirty in the afternoon. Gerfaut headed for the Porte d'Italie and got onto the Autoroute du Sud, the superhighway to the Mediterranean.

"Where the fuck is the prick going?" fumed Carlo.

It was the second of July, and people were still leaving on vacation. The traffic was jammed up all the way to Orly airport. Thereafter it thinned out somewhat, moving faster and more dangerously. Gerfaut did not bear right in the direction of Orléans but continued on toward Lyons.

"This is crazy. Where's he going now?" A note of genuine anxiety inflected Carlo's fury.

"I agree with you on that," said Bastien. "I think we go now."

"Go now? What the hell does that mean, 'go now'?"

"Pull up alongside," replied Bastien.

Carlo calmed down instantly. He even lifted his foot slightly from the gas pedal. The distance between the Lancia and the Taunus began to grow, soon surpassing five hundred meters.

"No! Never on the highway. That's the rule. No, my friend. Shit, a highway is an absolute trap."

"Suppose we wait till just before an exit," White Streaks suggested. "We ram him and get off right away."

"Right. And at the exit we run straight into motorcycle cops. You really are a dumb shit."

"That's not what you usually say."

"Give me a fucking break, okay?"

Bastien fell silent.

Just as night was falling, Gerfaut abruptly left the highway. Because of the delays near Paris they were only now approaching Mâcon. The two hit men had not eaten dinner. Nor had Gerfaut. The Taunus went through Mâcon and forged southwest. For a brief moment its sidelights came on. As yet, the Lancia had none of its lights on. Carlo was leaning forward slightly in his seat, his eyes narrowed. He drove fast. The distance between the Taunus and the Lancia had shrunk. Then one of the Lancia's tires blew out. The Italian car wove back and forth from one side of the road to the other. Carlo clung tightly to the wheel, teeth clenched, and uttered not a sound. Bastien jammed his head onto the headrest and crossed his arms across his face. The blown tire, left rear, swelled and began to shred. Its temperature rose violently. A cloud of white smoke rose behind the Lancia, and the stink of burnt rubber filled the car. Eventually, as Carlo shifted down into second, the vehicle rolled onto the right shoulder and came to rest in a gravel pile. Carlo and Bastien leaped from the car, cursing wildly, especially Carlo. They got out the jack and the spare tire. The taillights of the Taunus had disappeared round a bend far ahead. Bastien took a flashlight from the glove compartment and held it on Carlo as he changed the tire in one minute and forty seconds.

"Let me drive," said Bastien.

He took the wheel. Carlo jumped in beside him. They fastened their seatbelts and pulled back onto the road without even throwing up any gravel. Bastien was a meticulous and scientific driver. He put on his sidelights and his headlights and drove as fast as he could. On a number of straight stretches, he got up to 160 kilometers per hour.

"We should be able to see him," said Carlo.

They were approaching a town. They could see its lights against the black background of the foothills of the Alps, which blocked the horizon. To their left, a freight train rattled along. On the right, a service station appeared, small but well illuminated. The Taunus was standing at the pumps. In shirtsleeves in front of the car, Gerfaut was stretching and clasping his lower back and drawing on a Gitane filter. Pumping the gas was a young man in a smart uniform and a red canvas hat. The gas station had opened only recently, which explained the attendant's impeccable manner and appearance. Nonplussed, Bastien stamped on the brake pedal. The Lancia halted with a horrible screech of tires just past the gas station exit. Gerfaut turned his head and saw the Lancia and, through its right front window, Carlo, who was looking straight at him. Wheeling, he reached through his car's open window and grabbed the Star from his jacket. Hastily and clumsily he released the safety on the automatic.

"Put your hands up!" he announced idiotically.

The Lancia turned on a dime and drove into the gas station via the exit. The car sprang toward Gerfaut, who pulled the trigger of the automatic. The Lancia's windshield exploded. At the same time, Gerfaut jumped back, stumbled, and fell hard against a coffee machine, bruising his back agonizingly. The bright red car bore down on him, rocking and pitching. Gerfaut fled for his life, but the Lancia swerved and accelerated, threatening to smash Gerfaut into the office window. Gerfaut pirouetted away, but the car's left headlight struck him glancingly on the buttock and catapulted him across the cement on his belly. The Lancia utterly demolished the office window. With a thunderous roar, huge pieces of broken plate glass, road maps, toolboxes, cans of oil, lightbulbs, and cartoony promotional figures made of wire and latex were hurled in every direction.

With gravel still clinging to his forehead and cheeks and his nose scraped raw, Gerfaut turned over onto his back. His buttock was horribly painful. He had lost the Star. He had no idea where the weapon had landed. He raised himself on his elbows and saw Carlo get out of the Italian car, on the side farther from him, holding the Smith & Wesson .45. Bastien reversed at top speed, heading for the attendant, who abandoned the pump and ran for the office. Carlo took aim at Gerfaut. The attendant lowered his head and butted Carlo and sent him sprawling into the debris of the window, the lightbulbs, the road maps, the figurines, and all the other debris. The tank of the Taunus was full, but the automatic pump was still delivering high-octane gasoline at full flow, and the fuel was flowing freely across the concrete. A long rivulet wended its way toward Gerfaut.

Bastien got out of the Lancia and shot the pump attendant in the back with the SIG automatic. The man fell on his face at the door to the office, pulled his knees up beneath him, and tried to get up. Still sitting amid the debris of the office window, Carlo brought his .45 up with both hands, placed it against the side of the attendant's face, and blew the man's head off.

"Shit! Shit!" said Carlo.

Gerfaut managed to get up. He had taken three steps toward the Taunus when White Streaks fired at him with the SIG. The projectile raked his skull, and he fell bluntly on his back with blood streaming over his face. Carlo got to his feet, ran toward the Lancia, and got behind the wheel. Gerfaut rolled about on the concrete.

"Finish that cunt off!" yelled Carlo.

Bastien tossed his head to get his white forelock out of his eyes and headed for Gerfaut. Gerfaut took his Criquet lighter from his shirt pocket and ignited the rivulet of high-octane gasoline. His hand and arm were badly burned in the process. Flames leapt instantly from the lighter to the Taunus, enveloping the automobile in seconds. Gerfaut bounded to his feet, flabbergasted to discover that he could stand and even run. He dashed toward the road. As he reached it, he had the impression that he was still being fired on. At that moment the gas tank of the Taunus blew up, and the blast hurled him across the road. He landed nose first in soft earth and turnip or potato leaves. Once more he got to his feet. Shouting meaninglessly, he turned to look back. He was much impressed to see the killer with the white streaks in his hair flaming like a tailor's dummy, prostrate on the concrete with his arms crossed at his chest. Every window smashed and tires smoking, the Lancia emerged phoenix-like from the flames and bounced back onto the road. The panic-stricken Gerfaut turned his back on the inferno and began running across the field, wrenching his ankles in the loose dirt. He ran blindly in the direction of the railroad tracks.

12

When Gerfaut half regained consciousness, he did not know if he was at home in Paris, or on vacation, or even perhaps at Liétard's place. He was lying on a hard surface in an almost completely dark enclosed space. Slivers of light shone weakly through the walls. A rhythmic rattle filled his ears. He dreamed he was shooting at a man with an automatic pistol. The rhythm jolted him regularly. Upon reflection, he decided that he was in a railroad car, a freight car. Reassured by this thought, he fell back asleep.

Some time later, the door of the car was very slightly open, making the interior visible. Between two crates bearing the handwritten legend HANDLE WITH CARE, a man was sitting on his heels facing Gerfaut. In silhouette the fellow resembled a bear or some other animal—a beaver, possibly. He was entirely shrouded in a sleeveless oilskin raincoat, or rather cape, such as might be used by a cyclist to protect not only the head and back but also the legs and a bulky backpack. The guy across from Gerfaut had neither bike nor backpack, however. The raincoat puffed out about him like a wigwam, making it impossible to make out the shape of his body. He wore a bowler hat that was green with mildew. His face was fairly young looking, but wrinkled and unshaven and dirty, and his teeth were rotten.

Gerfaut himself was not a pretty sight. Grime and coagulated blood streaked his face. His shirt was ripped at the elbow, his pants at the knee and the seat. From head to toe he was splattered with mud, and his shoes were completely caked in it. Within his matted hair a bright red slash resembling a buttonhole could be seen, a piece of hairy scalp dangling from it onto his forehead.

"Do you work for French Railways?" Gerfaut asked.

The man made no reply and kept on looking at Gerfaut and grinning—unless this was the natural aspect of his face in repose. Gerfaut considered repeating his question at the top of his voice, in case the noise of the still-moving train had prevented the guy from hearing him. But that was unlikely, and Gerfaut felt weak, so he remained silent. A sudden thought caused him to start hunting through his pockets. His burned hand hurt. His whole body hurt. His gestures grew more and more frantic as he checked every pocket. He looked at the man with an injured expression, at first incredulous and then outraged. He made as if to get up. The drifter, for that was what he was, leapt to his feet instantly, drew back a flap of his oilskin cape and struck Gerfaut on the side of the head with a hammer. Gerfaut fell back onto the floor of the wagon. Once again he felt blood trickling across his skin. He could not get up. The drifter kicked him twice in the ribs. Raging, Gerfaut cried out and tore at the floor with his fingernails. The drifter watched him dispassionately or perhaps with amusement—it was impossible to tell what went on behind that awful fixed grin. The man's head was slightly tilted beneath the bowler hat, his right arm slightly bent, held slightly away from his body; he was ready to pull back the oilskin cape so as to hit Gerfaut again unimpeded. Then he opened the wagon's sliding door a little wider with his left hand, which required some effort.

Gerfaut had managed to shift his position somewhat. Blood trickled along the line of his lower jaw and dripped from his chin and splashed in tiny stars on the dusty floor in front of him. Things were happening in slow motion.

"You bastard! My wallet! My money! My checkbook!"

Through the open door of the freight car, Gerfaut could see

the tops of larch trees filing by. The track must have been elevated, or perhaps it ran along a mountainside, for the passing treetops seemed level with the wagon door. The drifter returned the hammer to his belt, grabbed Gerfaut under the armpits with his two hands, pulled him up, and, thrusting him forward, propelled him (as Gerfaut wailed incredulously) out of the car. For a moment Gerfaut's heel caught on the edge of the door, then he fetched up belly first in the ballast. All the breath was knocked out of him. He bounced, performing a somersault just as he had in the water when they had tried to drown him. Among the larches now, he rebounded and twirled on down the slope for fifty or sixty meters. Once again he lost consciousness. And he broke his foot.

13

In the late afternoon it began to rain. By now, Gerfaut was several kilometers from the railroad.

After his fall he had remained unconscious for but a few minutes. Picking himself up, he was amazed to discover that he was not dead. In truth, he was not really amazed. The events of the last few days, coming after a comfortable childhood and an early youth of successful upward mobility, had more or less convinced him that he was indestructible. But, given his improbable situation, arrived at by way of such thrilling vicissitudes, he found it appropriate, even exhilarating, to be surprised at the fact of still being alive. The image he now had of himself drew on a crime novel he had read some ten years earlier and from a small, baroque Western he had seen the previous fall at the Olympic movie theater. He had forgotten the titles of both works. In the first, a man left for dead and hideously mutilated by a crime boss proceeds to wreak a horrifying vengeance upon the said crime boss and his lackeys. In the film, Richard Harris is likewise left for dead by John Huston, but survives, living in a completely savage state, hating God and fighting with wolves for morsels of food.

Gerfaut shuddered at the thought of fighting ferocious animals for morsels of food.

Once he had come round and sat up, Gerfaut first leaned against the trunk of a larch and palpated himself with an excess of precaution. His left foot was painful. With the help of the tree trunk, he struggled to his feet. His foot gave way beneath him, and he slipped back to the ground, scraping his palms on the bark of the tree as he did so. A second attempt met with more success. He let go of the trunk he was holding on to and made it in four stiff and risky steps to another, around which he threw his arms, about three meters away. He experienced a sharp pain in his instep, but oddly it seemed to diminish when he walked. His ankle kept twisting painfully beneath his weight. Staggering from trunk to trunk, he nevertheless advanced fairly easily.

The slope helped him. Initially, he had wanted to make his way back to the railroad tracks in the hope of flagging down the next train or else following the rails to the nearest station. But he had to abandon this idea because of the steepness of the terrain. So he went downward, instead. The farther down into the valley you go, he told himself, the more likely you are to find houses. By and large, anyway.

One tree at a time, he cut across sharply falling land that supported a fine dark grass, mosses, and the odd cluster of mountain primrose, catchfly, or houseleek. The larch needles were slippery underfoot, and another barrier to quick progress were the many gullies of reddish earth strewn with loose stones. Gerfaut fell often. To go in the direction he had chosen, he was obliged to walk with his injured foot lower than the other on the slope, which made things much more difficult.

The air was crisp. The forest was full of lively, whispering breezes. Birds were few, darting with precision from tree to tree, just below the lowest branches. Once, looking up between the pistachio-green treetops, Gerfaut noticed a larger bird gliding high against a sky become gray. Soon afterward, he got beaten up all over again when he careened down into a ravine on the seat of his pants, bouncing and swearing as he went. As he finally came to rest, his ankle collided brutally with a tangle of roots, and he almost wept. Getting up yet again, and seeing where his slide had brought him, he thought he was done for.

So far down had he fallen that he was at the very bottom of a mud-filled hollow full of vegetable matter in various stages of decay. If there were wild boars at this altitude (which Gerfaut doubted), the place would surely have been a boar's lair. At all events, if Gerfaut was to go on in any direction at all, he would now have to climb.

He made several false starts that ended in pathetic and painful tumbles. At last, he had the idea of crawling and using his fingers for purchase. In this way, he dragged himself up a short incline and reached ground that was all broken up and distinctly discouraging: nothing but sharp rises, patches of bare granite, tangled branches brought down by lightening or avalanche, and vertiginous overhangs. From an aesthetic point of view, the landscape was highly romantic. From Gerfaut's point of view, it was absolute shit.

He continued to make headway, still on his belly, but his strength was on the ebb. Above, the sky was lowering. Then it began to rain.

It rained hard and long. Yellow water ran down the red gullies. Gerfaut hauled himself to a chaos of uprooted trees, curled up beneath them, and turned his shirt collar up. Water trickled between the fallen tree trunks and into his clothes. It was cold. Gerfaut began crying softly. Night fell.

At the break of day he had been asleep for only a short time. Anxiety, and a certain morose enjoyment of his misery, had kept him awake for many hours. Showers had followed one another at short intervals. Even when rain was not falling, water continued to run down the hillside, dripping from the branches above, percolating into Gerfaut's niche under the fallen trees and soaking him. When he opened his eyes, he felt as if he had only just closed them. His teeth were chattering. His grimy forehead was burning. He felt his injured foot and found it swollen and more painful than the day before. Laboriously he removed his mud-encrusted city shoe. When he stripped off his cotton sock, it ripped at the heel and instep. With a perverse satisfaction, Gerfaut contemplated the inflamed and purple flesh and the large, hard, unhealthy-looking protuberances on the front and side of his foot. He was unable to get his shoe back on, even after he tore out the lace and hurled it away from him with all his strength; it landed in the mud all of two meters away. He wanted to consult his Lip watch—which he had bought directly from the Lip workers when they had occupied their factory and which had never worked very well—but he discovered that he no longer had it. Then he recalled having already discovered this shortly after falling from the freight train.

The clouds no longer formed a uniform and somber vault. They had lost altitude and broken up on the mountainside. Gerfaut even saw some passing below him and reckoned that he must be at two or three thousand meters. He crawled out of his den on all fours. For five or six minutes he advanced furiously, ignoring the pain. He grunted like an animal—not without a measure of satisfaction.

This brief effort exhausted him utterly. Thereafter he took long, panting halts, moving forward only five or six meters between each. The weather had turned fair. The larches had thinned out. The sun started beating down madly. Steamy mist rose among the trees. Flying insects filled the air. Soon it was very, very hot. Gerfaut was burning up with fever. The whole business no longer gave him the feeling that he was in a novel.

As the day wore on and absolutely nothing in the situation changed, Gerfaut became frankly serious. He laid plans for long-term survival alone. He inventoried his possessions, which now comprised a dirty handkerchief, the keys to his Paris apartment, a scrap of squared paper bearing the telephone number of LTC Laboratories in Saint-Cloud, and six soaked Gitane filters in a crumpled pack. No lighter, no means of making a fire, no weapon, nothing to eat. Yet somehow Gerfaut got his second wind. He contrived to tear off a half-broken low branch of a tree and use it as a crutch. He began once more to walk on his two feet and even achieved a speed of four kilometers an hour. He entertained, then rejected, the idea of finding bees, following them back to their hive, somehow chasing away the swarms, and gorging on the honey. He decided that he would be stung countless times and put out of action once and for all—or die right then, for that matter. Besides, there were no bees anywhere to be seen.

He felt duty bound to sample every likely looking plant he noticed along the way in case it was edible. Everything he tried was hopelessly stringy or far too bitter.

Once, sitting on the ground, he hurled a fragment of granite at the head of a speckled brown bird that was clinging to a tree trunk and pecking at it. He missed his target by a wide margin without even frightening the creature. He didn't try a second shot.

The sun had dropped in the sky, and it must have been five or six by the time Gerfaut, still on his feet but advancing now at no more than two kilometers an hour, emerged into a meadow. He had earlier crossed a couple of clearings, spots where there were no more damned larches for thirty, maybe as much as fifty meters, but they had still blocked his view. This was different: even before reaching the forest's edge, Gerfaut saw thin grass extending a good hundred meters to a bluff. Beyond was a panoramic view of a great trough of a valley, bounded by wooded humped-back hills and ending some eight or ten kilometers away, in a low notch. On one flank of the valley was an area where the forest had been cleared. Higher up, just beyond the tree line, a pale shape indicated a shelter for hikers or possibly a cowshed.

Gerfaut immediately lost all sense of being lost in thousands of kilometers of wilderness. He hastened toward the outcrop, which hid the bottom of the valley from view. As he proceeded, he was thrilled to make out paths, other cleared areas, other cowsheds on the peaks.

As Gerfaut reached the end of the meadow, a joyful groan rose in his throat. Below his feet lay a little dark-blue lake and a fairly substantial town—more than two dozen houses with slate roofs, enclosures, dividing walls, roads, and straight, shimmering streaks that must have been some kind of giant hydraulic system for distributing water from the mountainside. Gerfaut was very thirsty. He stretched out slowly and heavily on his stomach to lick the grass and contemplate his good fortune.

A full minute passed before it occurred to Gerfaut that he was not yet home and dry. He calculated the distance between his position and the bottom of the valley. As the crow flies, one or two kilometers. On foot, perhaps five or even ten times that.

Horribly aggravated, Gerfaut rested for a moment or two. Then he became afraid of falling asleep and dying where he lay. He clambered to his feet with the aid of his makeshift crutch and set off again. In order to make the descent to civilization, he had to go back into the woods. At once he lost sight of the village. After a quarter of an hour of hesitant progress, he was hit by waves of anxiety that tightened his throat and his empty stomach at the thought that he might never find the houses or that it might require a week's march to reach them.

Night fell—for the second time since Gerfaut had been thrown from the train. He felt his way forward in the darkness. He collided with tree after tree. He wept. After falling twice, he gave up. He was very tired. Sleep came instantly. The next morning, he was found by a Portuguese logger.

14

At two in the morning, while Gerfaut was plunged in a comatose slumber, Radio Luxembourg announced that the Taunus had been identified. It was described as a vehicle rented the same day as the gas-station drama by Georges Gerfaut, a Parisian mid-level manager, who had since gone missing. Listeners were reminded that a service-station attendant and another man whose identity was still unknown had been killed on the evening of the second of July. As always on Radio Luxembourg during the night, the newsreader spoke in a neutral and low-key tone. In the same tone he reported on the situation in the Near East, on an attack on the Yugoslav embassy in Paris, and on a tragic drowning in the Loire (two children at some camp had lost their lives, along with a priest who had been in charge of them and who had gone to the rescue). The news was followed by a promotional spot for a concert sponsored by the station. Then came station identification, followed by Leonard Cohen.

It was hot. Wearing only baggy white underwear and white ankle socks, Carlo was sitting at the table in a room at the Hotel Saint-Jacques. His features were drawn and his eyes red rimmed; he looked like a man who had been weeping for a long time. He sat still and showed no reaction to the news bulletin. At the same time, he held the table tightly and performed isometric muscle-building exercises.

After the fire at the service station and the death of Bastien, Carlo had driven haphazardly, utterly stricken and sick with rage and self-recrimination. On the outskirts of Bourg-en-Bresse he had stopped to have an emergency windshield installed—a sheet of pliable plastic held in place by clips. He had thought things over and consulted maps. Then he set off again in the direction of Paris. He had been careful not to pass by the gas station, which was sure by now to be crawling with firefighters and police. Once back on the highway, he had stayed in the slow lane and never driven faster than seventy kilometers per hour. He had exited at Achères-la-Forêt around five in the morning. Somewhere in the forest of Fontainebleau he had pulled off the road and parked under the trees. Since he could not bury Bastien's body as he would have wished, he had taken the man's personal possessions from the metal suitcase and buried them—the nylon cord, the toilet bag, the clothes. The sight of Bastien's spare khaki underpants moved Carlo to tears—which tears rolled down his cheeks as he finished interring the objects and stamped down the loose earth to make it even. He had then sought words to pronounce over this pseudo-grave in lieu of a funeral oration. He could recall no prayer except for "Our Father." From the floor of the Lancia he retrieved an old issue of *Spiderman* (not to be confused with The Spider, whose adventures appear in *Strange* magazine). He had brightened at this, returned to the grave, opened the comic book, and begun with great solemnity to read the text that introduces every Spiderman adventure and which never varies: *Before becoming a righter of wrongs and a pitiless meter-out of justice, Spiderman reigned for years over the underworld of the USA as a veritable emperor of crime. Spiderman himself perfected a fabulous armamentarium that allows him to hold any criminal gang at bay. Spiderman also enlisted the services of two scientific geniuses, Professor Pelham and Professor Erichstein. So he has technical resources at his disposal that the ordinary human brain can barely imagine.*

Carlo lowered his head, closed the comic book, and meditated for a moment.

"Amen," he said. "So be it. I will avenge you, I swear this. I'll waste that motherfucker. *Ite missa est.*"

He returned to the Lancia, started it up, and got back on the road. He returned to Paris through the suburbs, taking his time. He stopped at a café in Viroflay and drank coffee and devoured six croissants. The coffee ran down his chin as he bit into the croissants.

At nine o'clock, at a garage he knew on the border between Meudon and Issy-les-Moulineaux, Carlo sold the Lancia. He could easily have had it fixed; the damage was not so great. But he preferred to sell the car at a loss because he wanted never to see it again; it reminded him too much of his life with Bastien and their happy partnership. Within the hour he had bought a plain 1973 Peugeot 504 two-door sedan, with 110 horsepower at 5,600 rpm and a top speed, in a pinch, of 175 kph; he also bought a set of realer-than-real fake identity papers in the name of Edmond Bron.

Then Carlo had returned to Paris, passing without knowing it by Liétard's photo shop near the Issy town hall, and taken a room at the Hotel Saint-Jacques. He had not budged since. He slept there, he ate there; only once had he gone out—to see a film showing in a theater on the ground floor of the hotel building. In his room he also did exercises, isometric or otherwise, but what he did mainly was mourn Bastien. And wait for things to cool down.

15

In point of fact, there was a whole campful of Portuguese log-gers less than fifty meters from Gerfaut when he stopped and fell asleep. Had he taken but a few more steps he would perhaps have come upon them; he might equally well have passed them by in the night without ever seeing them.

The particular Portuguese logger who stumbled upon Gerfaut had not gone very far at all from the camp, having stepped away to piss or something of that order. The man was tall and robust, dark in complexion but clean shaven, with prominent yellow teeth. He wore dark gray herringbone trousers and a cheap Jacquard pullover that was too small for him and patched at the elbows; it had once been white with a red motif, but repeated washing had turned the whole thing a filthy pink color. A floppy black beret completed the picture. The Portuguese came over and contemplated Gerfaut, who at that moment opened his eyes and returned the man's stare.

"Good morneen," said the Portuguese in badly mangled French. He licked his lips and smiled.

Gerfaut responded as best he could to the salutation and tried to get up, but he fell back on the ground. He felt extremely weak, ill, and tired.

"Thirsty," he mumbled.

"Oh, yes," said the Portuguese. "Slip all night here, yes?" (The man pointed to the ground.) "Very cull."

"What?"

"Cull! Very cull! No hot," the man explained to Gerfaut, who seemed very rattled. "You want vino, yes?"

"Vino, sí," replied Gerfaut, nodding vigorously. "Habla

español?" The logger's response was vague. "Yo perdido. Muy malo. Cold."

"Yes, cull," went the man.

"Achoo!" said Gerfaut, and to stress the point he made a gesture indicating that he was coming down with bronchitis (which is easier than might be supposed).

The Portuguese helped Gerfaut to his feet and led him to the campsite. Along the way, still convinced that his interlocutor understood Spanish, Gerfaut kept offering useless interjections such as "Qué mala suerte!" and "Qué barbaridad!" while pointing to his swollen foot or his blood-scabbed forehead.

There were eight loggers, encamped beneath a canvas sheet held up by stakes. Their blankets were filthy, and they slept on bundled branches and leaves. They had stale bread, a little Algerian wine, cheese, bad coffee, big sacks of dried peas and beans, and three magazines filled with obscene photographs. Their professional equipment consisted of axes and saws and two Homelite chain saws. Their presence in France was illegal, they had no kind of social security, and they earned only slightly more than half the minimum wage for some sixty to seventy hours of work per week. They gave Gerfaut bread and pea soup, and two doses of powdered aspirin dissolved in wine. They didn't know what to do with him. As he was shivering and sweating terribly, they rolled him up in a couple of smelly blankets.

"Someone will be coming," the logger with the best French told Gerfaut.

Then the men picked up their axes, their handsaws, and their Homelites and disappeared among the trees. The morning light was rather splendid, for those who like that sort of thing. Bronchitis or not, swollen foot or not, Gerfaut would likely have been physically able to resume his journey to the valley bottom, and he considered the possibility after the loggers had been gone for over two hours. But his moral fiber had weakened momentarily—ever since he had been found, ever since he had been taken care of.

He waited for the lunch hour, listening hard for the distant sound of the chain saws, but was unable to decide whether this was what he could hear or whether it was merely the wind in the branches. He dragged himself across the ground and picked up the girlie magazines. The text was in English and very poor, not just from the literary point of view but even in terms of sexual fantasy. As for the pictures, they were of corpulent women with vulgar, even brutal features. Gerfaut's taste was more sophisticated, inclining him more toward scrawny women with high cheekbones. Inasmuch, that is, as his taste could be said to incline him toward anything at all. He turned to the readers' letters. A single great debate informed the magazine's columns: big breasts versus big asses. To Gerfaut this seemed like a false problem. He was bored silly.

About ten-thirty, he had tossed the magazines away and was feeling infinitely wretched and ill, indeed almost at death's door, when one of the Portuguese loggers reappeared, bringing with him an old man in a hat. Long white hair fell to the old man's shoulders and over his brown wide-wale corduroy jacket. He greeted Gerfaut with a grunt and knelt down beside him. Throwing back the blankets in which Gerfaut was bundled, he rolled up his left pants leg and examined and palpated his bad foot.

"Do you speak French? Who are you?" Gerfaut's questions drew no response. The old man went on manipulating Gerfaut's foot with the fixed concentration of a truffle pig.

"But tell me, at least," cried Gerfaut feebly, overcome by anxiety and confusion, "I'm in France, aren't I? These are the Alps, surely?"

The old man dug his fingers into Gerfaut's inflamed flesh and exerted a vigorous twisting pressure. Gerfaut screamed. Tears burst through his tightly closed eyelids and streaked his grubby bearded jowl. He ground his bared teeth. He raised his elbows from the ground and tried to touch his ankle, but the old man thrust him away and Gerfaut fell flat on his back. From his jacket pocket the old man produced a Nescafé can, which he opened. It held a viscous yellow paste that looked to Gerfaut like axle grease. The man took a generous handful of the stuff and smeared it over Gerfaut's instep, which he then massaged energetically.

"Yes, of course you're in the Alps. Of course you're in France. What's the matter with you? You're in La Vanoise, that's where you are."

"You're a bonesetter?"

"I don't care for that word. I'm a military nurse. So what happened to you? You're a tourist, huh? Shouldn't be running up hill and down dale with a foot in this condition." He applied a square of gauze to Gerfaut's instep and began winding a stretch bandage around his foot.

"I fell from a train."

"I've set the bones straight," said the old man. "I am Corporal Raguse. What train? What is your name?"

"Georges," answered Gerfaut. "Georges Sorel," he added hastily. "I fell from a freight train the other night. I'm a vagabond. Do you understand? I'm on the railroad. Not a railroad worker—I travel on the railroad. I'm a tramp." Gerfaut was out of breath by the time he had said all this.

Corporal Raguse stood up wiping his hands on a purple-check handkerchief. He started putting everything he had taken out back in his pockets: the can of ointment and the containers for the gauze dressings and crepe bandages—flat, oblong tin boxes, not a little rusty, with hinged lids.

"You shouldn't be moved at all before tomorrow. These Portuguese will take care of you. They are good people. Tomorrow morning I'll come for you with a mule."

"Another night here? But I am ill," protested Gerfaut.

"Don't argue. Drink some wine."

"I have no money."

"I don't do this for money," said Raguse. "I do this to help my fellow man."

16

Corporal Raguse had long since left the military and indeed had never been a corporal. He could barely be said to have been a soldier at all. Too young for the First, he was almost too old for the Second World War. He had nevertheless acquired some nursing and mule-driving skills while waiting six months for an improbable Italian attack. He had used firearms only during the German occupation and very rarely against human targets. The whitewashed room where he put Gerfaut after fetching him with his mule was oddly decorated with a portrait of Stalin and one of Louis Pasteur (the latter, in reality, being a photograph of Sacha Guitry playing Pasteur in an old film). Gerfaut spent a week in bed in that room, reading the *Vermot Almanac,* Maurice Maeterlinck's *Life of the Bee,* and the startling autobiography of one Father Bourbaki, missionary and aviator. Gerfaut's imagination was especially piqued by the part of this last work wherein the bloodthirsty cleric, between two bouts of *boche*-killing, tried to solve a problem concerning his pennant. A tricolor adorned by the sacred heart of Christ, this pennant was continually ripping on account of the speed of the black-beetle-cum-warrior's airplane, to whose bracing wire the thing was attached. Bourbaki eventually solved his problem by laminating the pennant in Muscovy glass. The remainder of the book, thronged by "leprous negroes," was tedious in the extreme.

Raguse had put Gerfaut's foot in plaster, and for the first few days he brought food to his bedside: in the morning, light coffee, fresh cheese, and a rotgut brandy that the former male nurse distilled himself from overripe fruit, notably pears and quinces; and, for both lunch and dinner, soup and bread, dried sausage with great blotches of rancid fat, cheese, sometimes mackerel in white wine from a long narrow can, and an acidic, light-colored red wine.

"You have to eat, Sorel," the Corporal would tell him. "Have to get your strength back. Your tissues have to repair themselves."

Before long, Gerfaut was able to hobble from his bedroom to the table of the main room. The Raguse house, built into the side of a hill away from the village, had mortarless stone walls and a slate roof. Inside, the walls were covered with a mud-and-sand roughcast and whitewashed. Large blocks of granite rested on the roof to ensure that the slates didn't fly off in a high wind. Properly speaking, it was a single-story house, but because of its hillside situation there was space beneath for a combination cellar and stable opening over the downslope. Here Raguse kept his bottles, his provisions, his still, and his mule. Above were the main room, with a very large fireplace and a basalt sink, and two bedrooms. The rooms had small windows with small panes and small wooden shutters with heart-shaped cutouts.

"I knew right away you weren't a real vagrant," said Raguse, his mouth full of cheese, pouring them both wine. They had just sat down to lunch. The massive table was thickly overlain with dirt. Glowing embers sputtered in the fireplace. An unkempt fair beard now covered Gerfaut's lower face. His injured foot was still weak. The wound on his scalp had healed, but a stripe of white would mark the spot amid Gerfaut's otherwise blond hair for the rest of his life.

"I dumped my wife. Yes, that's it—that's what I did."

"I'm not asking you anything. Come with me."

His mouth still full of cheese, his felt hat on his head, the old man got to his feet with a grunt, closed his Opinel knife with a guillotine-like snap, and thrust it into his jacket pocket. He then went toward his bedroom. At a loss for words, Gerfaut got up too and quickly drained his glass.

"Can you shoot, Sorel?"

"What?"

"Shoot," repeated Raguse, disappearing into his room.

Gerfaut followed him. It was the first time he had set foot in Raguse's room, which scarcely differed from his own. Old furniture, metal bedstead—just the same. A post-office calendar offered a nighttime view of the Champs-Elysées. On a shelf stood a frame aerial for a radio receiver—though no radio was to be seen anywhere in the place. It incorporated a hideously tinted portrait of Martine Carol. There was a large chest. A wardrobe. And a gun rack holding a double-barreled Falcor, a Charlin, and a Weatherby Mark V rifle with Imperial sights. Raguse took down the Weatherby.

"Well, we'll just see."

"I'm not some kind of crook on the run, if that's what you're thinking."

"I know that, son."

Raguse had opened the chest and taken out ammunition, which he was now loading into the weapon. This done, he plunged his hand back into the chest, where folded fabrics could be seen, along with rusty tins, assorted boxes, tools, and the like. He produced a pair of binoculars. The two men left the room, then the house. Gerfaut limped along with his plaster. The sunshine made him dizzy. Raguse took a few steps, then indicated the grassy slope that rose behind the house toward the forest above. He narrowed his dark eyes, which all but disappeared in the folds of flesh. He looked irritable now, pained.

"There has to be an empty green-pea can on a stick about a

hundred meters up there. Can you see it, young fellow?"

"No. Oh, wait a second. Yes, maybe."

Raguse passed the gun to Gerfaut. "Make sure there's no-body about and take a shot at it."

The old man brought the glasses up to his eyes, paying no further attention to Gerfaut. Far from comfortable in his role, Gerfaut awkwardly fitted the weapon into his shoulder. In the sights, once he had properly brought them to bear, he could see his target clearly. He aimed as best he could. When he pressed the trigger nothing happened; he had omitted to release the safety. He released it and tried again. The gun went off, but he missed the can and couldn't even see a point of impact.

"Ridiculous," declared Raguse without lowering the binocu-lars. "Imagine you're shooting at something you want to hit, young fellow. An animal, whatever you want. A guy."

Gerfaut pulled back the bolt, his gaze fixed on the ground, and accidentally ejected a new cartridge. Then he took aim again carefully, held his breath, and blew a large hole in the green-pea can at a hundred meters.

They went back to the house.

"A very fine gun," said Gerfaut politely, handing the Weatherby back to the old man so he could clean it and put it back in its place.

"You said it!" cried the old man. "It's worth its weight in gold. A German it was that gave it to me, twelve years ago. I saved his life, more or less. A hunter. I found him with a leg bust to blazes—a bit like you, but it was higher up."

"I'm going to have to leave here soon."

Raguse looked at Gerfaut sharply.

"I'm not looking for payment. I have everything I need. My granddaughter sends me money every month, and I don't even spend it all. I put it in the savings bank in Saint-Jean. I don't need a thing. If what you're thinking, young fellow, is that you have to go off and earn money just to pay me for my trouble, you can think again."

"I can't spend the rest of my life here."

"Till I take the plaster off, you're as well off here as anywhere. Then, if this place is not to your liking...."

"Not at all," Gerfaut hastened to reply. "I like it fine here."

"You can help out," said Raguse with enthusiasm. "Have you ever hunted?"

Gerfaut shook his head. Raguse returned the Weatherby to the gun rack and closed his chest. They went back into the main room.

"Hunting is my only pleasure," said Raguse, looking sly and boyish now. "The National Forest of La Vanoise can kiss my ass," he declared contentedly. "But I can't see clearly anymore. Once I get that plaster off, perhaps you'll help me. We can go hunting together, and you can be my extra pair of eyes, as you might say."

"Why not?" answered Gerfaut with an affable smile—was it a derisive smile or a plain dumb smile? "Why not? I'm no use anymore. I'm nowhere. Lost. I might as well be someone's extra pair of eyes."

That night Gerfaut had nightmares with Béa and the girls in them, and the two killers in their red car, and Baron Frankenstein transporting glass jars filled with extra pairs of eyes.

At the beginning of September, Gerfaut's plaster started falling apart of its own accord. Raguse finished the job. Gerfaut was greatly relieved to be able at last to scratch his foot. He still limped a little, and the old man muttered that it would never straighten itself out, and Gerfaut said that he could care less.

Then Raguse rooted in his old chest and began poring over greasy old manuals with bindings crumbling away by themselves. They had anatomical drawings of men with mustaches. The Corporal gave Gerfaut an exercise program to be followed every day in order to reduce his limp and, above all, to obviate any possible misalignment of the spinal cord or of other bones.

Gerfaut made himself useful by running little errands in the village; he would pick up tobacco, for instance, or Riz la Croix cigarette papers, or lighter fluid when the need arose. Occasionally, at the café-tabac, he would glance through the regional paper, *Le Dauphiné Libéré*, to see what was happening in the world. Sporting events took up as much space as ever. Third World riots, famines, floods, epidemics, assassinations, palace revolutions, and local wars still followed one another in quick succession. In the West the economy was not working well, mental illness was rife, and social classes were still locked in struggle. The Pope deplored the unrestrained hedonism of the age.

After a brief period of natural curiosity, the villagers, old for the most part and less numerous than the houses, were content to accept a few half-truths and stopped asking Gerfaut questions. In the past, Corporal Raguse had taken in injured animals, lodged stray hikers, and allowed British campers to pitch tents in the meadow behind his house. Gerfaut seemed like just another of his broken wings, a taciturn semi-vagrant, a bit simple but serviceable enough, who gave the old man a hand. He even helped the local police shove their vehicle out of the mud one time when they had ventured this far up the mountainside during an early-autumn rainstorm. On another occasion, he had paid for a round of drinks at the café-tabac, then told his troubles: his wife had left him; he had once been

a manager in a big firm, but he had left everything behind—
just as a lot of people did, so it was said, in America: they become *dropahoutes.*

"A *dropahoute,* yes, that's it!" said Gerfaut. "That's me exactly! Cheers, everybody!" And he emptied his glass.

When fall came, Raguse began getting Gerfaut used to long
mountain walks. These became longer and longer, and after a
few weeks the two men took guns with them and the walks
turned into hunting trips.

Usually, they rambled in the wooded area. From time to
time, they would bag game birds: partridge, plover, hazel
grouse, capercaillie, or else a squirrel or hare. Raguse, whose
eyesight had become really poor, missed everything he took
aim at. After a time, he virtually gave up shooting altogether
and let Gerfaut take over.

One day in late October, with the Weatherby, Gerfaut and
Raguse climbed higher than they ever had before. There had
been a few snowfalls, then milder weather had returned. They
crossed the forest and went up through the mountain pastures
with their bilberry patches and clumps of rhododendrons.
Granite crags and snowy hillocks soon defined their whole horizon. The two men followed the rock-strewn path upward.
The old man seemed delighted. Gerfaut's feelings were amor-
phous. Indeed, for as long as he had been on the mountainside
he had remained in a kind of stupor. At this moment, he contemplated the scenery without finding it either beautiful or
ugly; he felt his bad leg protest but gave no thought to pausing;
sweat trickled down his back and over his rib cage, the wind
raked his face, but he paid these things no mind.

In mid-afternoon they halted at a stone refuge with wooden
partitions, a hearth, and charcoal inscriptions on the rock of

the interior walls; hikers had clearly wanted to leave a trace of their visit to a place so high above sea level. Gerfaut felt no such compulsion. They carried on, and an hour later Raguse, whose enfeebled vision the Weatherby's sights made up for quite effectively, succeeded for once in bringing down a horned animal at some four hundred meters. Whether a chamois or an ibex Gerfaut had no idea, for he didn't know the difference; it might as well have been an antelope or a snail—he didn't give a damn. They went to retrieve the carcass and spelled each other dragging it downhill. By the time they got home, it was darkest night. Raguse was producing an endless stream of taunts and obscenities directed at the National Forest of La Vanoise and its gamekeepers. Gerfaut never did try to discover the motive for the old man's animus.

During the night they cut up their prize. They salted quarters. The hide was set aside, as was the halved head. In the days following, Raguse set about tanning the one and stuffing the other.

"I'll sell them to idiots. They can stick them in their drawing rooms."

"What in God's name am I doing here?" asked Gerfaut irritably. "Can you please tell me that?" He had just downed several healthy tots of fruit brandy; these days he was drinking more and more heavily. "I spend my time doing sweet fuck-all."

"Look here, Sorel. You can leave, you know. Any time you want. You're a free man."

"Yes," said Gerfaut, "but it's the same shit everywhere."

By and large, though, Gerfaut got on pretty well with the old man. They went on more expeditions. On other days, and more and more often now that the cattle had come down from the Alpine pastures and been returned to their cowsheds,

Raguse was called on for veterinary help, and Gerfaut would go along to give him a hand, hold the lamp, and the like. He learned how to grasp a cow's horns and force her head down so that Raguse could remove a foreign body from the beast's eye, which he did with the help of a butter-soaked feather or sometimes merely by flinging powdered sugar into the eye, causing it to water so violently that the irritant was washed out. This was just about all Gerfaut learned.

In early April, with the cold and the bad weather hanging on, a night came when Raguse, after tying one on, caught a wicked cold. Around midnight he called for Gerfaut and announced that he was going to die. Being three sheets to the wind himself, Gerfaut took this as a joke. But, when dawn came, Raguse was dead.

17

"I didn't picture you the way you are," Gerfaut said to Alphonsine Raguse.

"How *did* you picture me?"

She was sitting in the main room, in the old man's easy chair. She wore pearl-gray corduroy slacks, brown ankle boots, an ecru sweater, and a brown leather coat. Her hair was very black, thick, healthy, and cut simply in the form of a German soldier's helmet by a hairdresser, the merest snip of whose scissors must have cost a packet of money. Her skin was perfectly smooth and tan, her eyes pale, her eyebrows set high, her cheekbones prominent, her nose of modest size, and her jaw determined. When she smiled, her red lips parted horizontally to reveal teeth as perfect and gleaming as one could wish. She resembled a very good ad for a vacation club (though ads for vacation clubs never actually look like that; they make you want to stay at home if at all possible). She was drinking vodka. She had brought the vodka along with her in her Ford Capri. She had also brought along a guy by the name of Max. At this moment, the guy had gone off again in the Capri to do some shopping about twenty-five kilometers away.

"Well, I don't really know," replied Gerfaut. "I suppose I imagined a woman about forty-five but looking older, with hands red from washing dishes and doing heavy work, and eyes red, too, from all the sad things that had happened to her. She would have got here by taxi and bus, wearing a moth-eaten black coat. But, my God—how old are you anyway? Oh, excuse me."

"Twenty-eight. No need to apologize."

"You can't be Raguse's daughter?"

"No, his granddaughter."

"Sometimes he used to mention a daughter who sent him money...."

"That was me."

"I see," said Gerfaut. "Forgive me. I don't know why I'm asking you all these questions. I have no right to. I'll be going now. Thank you for the drink."

He rose from his stool to put the mustard glass from which he had been drinking vodka in the basalt sink.

"You are not from around here," she said. "You're a Parisian."

"Originally, yes," said Gerfaut. He was amused by the question, and he smiled beneath his blond beard. "You would never believe it if I told you how I ended up here."

"You could give it a try."

Gerfaut chuckled. He felt like a kid.

"It's quite simple, really. Until last summer I was a middle manager in a company in Paris. I went on vacation, and two men tried to kill me, twice, for reasons unknown to me. Two complete strangers. At which point I left my wife and children and, instead of informing the police, I fled. I found myself in a freight car crossing the Alps. A drifter knocked me down with a hammer and threw me off the train. I injured my foot, which is why I limp now. Your father, or rather your grandfather, found me and cared for me. That's it."

In the easy chair the young woman was laughing uproariously.

"That's the simple truth," said Gerfaut. He was having trouble keeping a straight face.

"Have another drink," said Alphonsine Raguse, waving vaguely toward the bottle of vodka. There was still a trace of irrepressible laughter in her voice, and her gray eyes were still watering. She wiped them and sighed. Gerfaut retrieved his mustard glass from the sink, wiped its base on his sleeve, and poured himself a little more vodka. He ran two fingers lightly through his hair.

"Suppose I told you that this is the mark of a bullet wound— this white tuft here?"

"Yes, sure," answered Alphonsine. "You are quite the adventurer."

"No, not at all. You don't understand. I'm just the opposite."

"What does that mean, the opposite?"

"Someone who doesn't remotely want adventures."

She was still smiling. Ironically—but not in a mean way.

"I wouldn't mind an adventure with you, though," Gerfaut blurted. "Oh, I'm so sorry. That's not what I meant to say. How embarrassing."

She fell silent for quite some time. A worried look came over her face. Gerfaut found no way of breaking the silence, and he didn't dare look at the woman. He felt dumb.

"How was the funeral?" she asked suddenly. "I didn't want to come. I'm not upset that my grandfather is dead. I don't like funerals. To like funerals you have to like death, and I don't see how anyone can like death. But no," she went on nervously, "that's stupid, what I just said. Lots of people love death. Actually, I don't know...."

She said no more, as though out of breath. She looked down at the floor. Under the suntan the skin of her face pinkened and then turned the color of a boiled lobster. She gave Gerfaut a hard look. She got to her feet, and Gerfaut politely followed suit. Then she slapped him viciously across the face—once, then again. Gerfaut failed to grab her wrist; he covered his face with his forearm and backed toward the wall.

"Forgive me, please forgive me," he said. He giggled slightly as his back bumped the wall. "It's because I've been for eight or ten months—the whole winter—in a sort of sexual stasis. Can you see what I mean?" He was mumbling—not even trying to make himself clear.

"Not me, though!" She was shouting; she stamped her foot, then kicked Gerfaut in the shin, hard. "Not me! I didn't spend the winter in a sort of sexual stasis, as you put it so snottily, Monsieur Sorel!"

They heard the Capri pull up in front of the house. Alphonsine turned her back on Gerfaut and went to the door, banging her heels as hard as she possibly could on the wooden floor as if she wanted to send shock waves to his brain. Gerfaut leaned against the wall and tried to relax by inhaling deeply (without overdoing it).

Alphonsine's boyfriend Max came in. He, too, banged his heels loudly on the floor, but in his case it was to get warm.

"Monsieur Sorel will be staying tonight," said Alphonsine in a placid, musical tone. "He'll be able to give us more information about the place."

"Fine, that's fine," said Max. He was about thirty-five or so, with dark hair and green eyes, and a triangular upper body—a good-looking guy, the sort to whom certain things come easily; he had on plaid pants and an elegantly grimy three-quarter-length suede coat over a white pullover. "But they've got a place to eat down there that doesn't seem too shitty. I really don't see why we have to go through all the hassle of cooking here."

"You have to inhabit a place, really live in it, if you want to know what it's like, what it—well, never mind." Alphonsine kissed Max on the mouth and rubbed briefly up against him in a provocative manner; and for the next few minutes she manifested submissiveness toward him in a host of ways. She did the cooking, barely giving Gerfaut the chance to explain a few things about the drain or how to manage without a stove. Only on sufferance were the two men permitted to feed the fire in the hearth and lay the table.

They ate dinner and chatted. Alphonsine allowed that she had decided to keep the house and make major improvements to it.

"Yes, yes," Max agreed enthusiastically. "What a fabulous place to come to—cut off from everything like this."

"My sweetheart." She caressed his elbow and nuzzled at his shoulder through the white pullover.

All the same, sitting across from the loving couple with his nose in his glass, Gerfaut caught the young woman looking at him in a way that was bright, ardent, unseemly, even slightly crazy.

Yet it would be quite some time before Alphonsine and Gerfaut fell upon each other and sought to possess each other. For the moment, the three spent the night at the house, Gerfaut alone in his room, where he slept badly, and the couple in the old man's room. The next morning Alphonsine asked Gerfaut rather imperiously to be the house's caretaker. She planned to go back to Paris, find an architect, and begin major alterations that would call for local construction people and craftsmen. And Gerfaut would oversee the work, which would be finished by summer. She would pay Gerfaut. She thought he would refuse the offer of payment, but he accepted it. Sure enough, she left the same day with her guy Max. But she came back well before the summer, and she came alone. Gerfaut was still there, caretaker-ing, seemingly without a care in the world.

Still, the day after the couple's departure he had lit the fire with a copy of the evening *France-Soir* from the day before, which the pair had left behind. By chance, as he scrunched the newspaper up into loose airy balls, his eye had fallen upon a very short article—no more than filler—headed "Possible New Light Thrown on Disappearance of Paris Executive Georges Gerfaut After Massacre of Last Summer," which was a very long title for such a brief item.

18

"You're not a cop," said the drifter.

"I'm a journalist," said the young man with wavy black hair and such pretty blue eyes, whose name was Carlo. "The drinks are on me, if you tell me something interesting."

"I told the cops everything, even an inspector that came down from Paris. I repeated everything over and over. Why don't you just ask them?"

The drifter had prominent yellow teeth and a deformed mouth that gave him a perpetual smirk. He wriggled, ill at ease, licked his lips, and mechanically adjusted his dirty bowler hat over his likewise dirty hair. He regretted no longer having his hammer. The young man with the dark hair took a money clip from the pocket of his navy-blue raincoat and extracted a fifty-franc bill. He waved it in front of the drifter, simultaneously rolling it up with three fingers like a cigarette. The drifter made an unconvincing grab for the money, then shook his head.

"Come on now," said Carlo in reproachful tones. He took a step forward, lifted the man's bowler and jammed the rolled banknote between his hat and his hair so that the money was attached to the drifter's forehead.

"Like I told the cops—" The man broke off and looked at Carlo uncertainly. But Carlo was waiting for the rest. The two were alone on the edge of a cornfield; night was falling, Carlo's Peugeot 504 was parked at the edge of a back road, a church steeple could be seen through the trees some two or three kilometers away, and there was nothing and nobody to call for help. The drifter saw no alternative to continuing, so he continued.

"Like I said to the cops, this checkbook belonging to Monsieur Gerfaut, I found it on the ground. At the Lyons railroad station—not the Lyons station in Paris, I mean the Perranche station in Lyons. It was six months ago or more, maybe even eight. I kept it because I thought I could go sometime and turn it in to a branch of the BNP Bank, because, you know, it was a checkbook from that bank, and pick up a little reward. Or, well, perhaps I thought I might use it myself, I won't deny that, but it's no crime just thinking about it, is it?" The drifter's fixed grin was even more noticeable—was he perhaps smiling nervously? "But I never did use it. I kept it, that's all. That's all I know—I swear it on my mother's grave."

The drifter said nothing more and tried to look at the money dangling down his forehead, which caused him to squint. He made no effort to touch it.

"You're reciting," said Carlo.

"Sure I am. They kept asking me the same thing, the cops. And that policeman from Paris. They beat me, monsieur—if you are a journalist, this should be of interest to you. They made me kneel on a steel ruler, and they were hitting me on the head all the time with telephone directories, and it went on for days and days. They got me sent down for thirty days, for vagrancy. In prison I was hassled again. They wanted me to change my story, but I can't change my story because it's the truth."

"You've got one more chance." Carlo was irritated.

"Can I sit down? I'm tired."

Carlo shrugged. The drifter bent his knees and subsided slowly and heavily onto his heels. Upon his release from prison his hammer had not been returned to him. But they had no right to confiscate it, because it was a tool of his trade, an all-metal hammer with a hollow shaft containing accessories such as screwdriver heads, a corkscrew, and an awl. But they had never given it back to him, and who was he to complain? Pretending to reach out to steady himself, he felt about on the ground with his right hand and his fingers closed over a flinty stone. He drew back his arm, meaning to smash it into Carlo's knee. But Carlo stepped swiftly aside, seized the moving arm and pulled it hard, twisting slightly as he did so. The drifter's shoulder dislocated with a sharp crack.

"Shithead!" said Carlo.

"Help! Help!"

Carlo kicked the drifter in the stomach. The man doubled up and quieted down because he could no longer shout. With his left hand Carlo sent the bowler flying and grabbed the drifter by the hair. He forced his head back and shook it. The fifty-franc bill fell into the grass and the dust and the gravel. Carlo reached into his raincoat pocket with his right hand and produced a Swiss Army knife.

"Look," he said to the drifter, still twisting his hair.

The drifter squeaked like a mouse as the other man stuck the knife into his side and he felt it being turned then withdrawn. Blood flowed abundantly.

"Do you get it?" Carlo asked. "I am not an ordinary cop. I'm a really brutal cop, okay? Now it's time to tell me the truth."

The drifter told the truth about how he had come by Georges Gerfaut's checkbook. It had no resemblance to what he had told the police or to what the press had reported (Carlo had the clippings in his wallet, including the *France-Soir* item entitled "Possible New Light Thrown," etc.). The younger man made quite sure he had extracted the whole story, then dragged the drifter to the middle of the cornfield and stove his skull in with a rock. He emptied his victim's pockets (haul: thirteen francs and seventy centimes) and relieved him of his down-at-heel shoes. Perhaps this would make things look like the outcome of a squabble between derelicts. Not that it made much difference. On his way back to the Peugeot, Carlo did not forget to retrieve the fifty-franc bill that had fallen on the ground.

19

Yes, it was indeed well before summer that Alphonsine Raguse returned. To be precise, it was the first of May, though it has to be said that, as firsts of May go, this was one of the lousiest of the decade as far as the weather was concerned. Rain fell over three-quarters of France, and an Atlantic storm drove great waves high over the shoreline way up the estuary of the Gironde, as, for instance, at Saint-Georges-de-Didonne; a veritable hurricane tore up the Seine valley, ripping off roofs at Magny-en-Vexin and beyond it, as in Paris, and, of course, short of it also, as at Vilneuil, a hamlet exactly thirty kilometers from Magny.

At Vilneuil, Alonso Emerich y Emerich was alarmed by the wind. He did not convey his alarm to Bastien or Carlo. In the past, he had on occasion apprised them of concerns of his (albeit concerns of another sort). For one thing, it was months since Alonso had had any contact with the two hit men; not since the Gerfaut fiasco, in fact. For another, Bastien was dead. And for yet another, Alonso had not the slightest idea what had become of Carlo or where he was now. In point of fact, Carlo was hundreds of kilometers away from Vilneuil, in a hotel room in Chambéry. He had had chicken sandwiches sent up, along with four bottles of German beer. The television was on, but the volume was muted. Carlo could easily afford a hotel with television in every room, for he had been given several contracts since Bastien's death. He was now used to working without his partner—used to working alone, in fact, since he had no plans to take on anyone else. Not that he had given up the idea of avenging Bastien, though he no longer wore a mourning band. At this very moment, in fact, he was ignoring

Armand Jammot on the television and studying his own hand-written notes concerning the timetables and routes of freight trains in the Alps. He was also perusing maps published by the National Geographical Institute at a scale of 1:25,000 covering a polygon whose points were Chambéry, Aix-les-Bains, Annecy, Chamonix, Val d'Isère, Briançon, and Grenoble. His task was a long one. As he proceeded, Carlo leaned into the wall or clasped the table tightly, performing his isometric muscle-strengthening exercises. In the metal suitcase on a baggage stand were a change of clothes, the S&W .45, the three knives and the steel, the garrote, the blackjack, and all the rest. Carlo's toilet bag was in the bathroom, and on the bedside table was a science-fiction novel by Jack Williamson in French translation. The canvas bag containing the over-and-under M6 and the binoculars lay on the floor against the wall.

As Carlo took his first bite of chicken sandwich, Alphonsine Raguse had already been in her grandfather's house for several hours. A thick fog blanketed the little valley. For some reason, the area escaped the ravaging wind. The mist hung in the still air like absorbent cotton laid across the ground.

Alphonsine and Gerfaut were having almost nonstop fun. Between the two of them, things were going well. They were delighted to have engaged at last in sexual congress and intended to repeat the experience as often as possible. At every moment they clasped fingers, caressed each other's shoulders or hair, kissed one another on the temple or in the crook of the arm; their eyes glistened; they were fragrant with sweat and other bodily fluids; they giggled frequently.

Gerfaut was at the table in the main room, shirtless and barefoot, wearing cotton pants that were too short for him. Before him on the table was an ITT portable radio receiver with a long, inclined antenna. A dessert plate did service as an ash-tray. Gerfaut held a Gitane filter. The radio was playing jazz, a Johnny Guarnieri piano solo, part of a program from France Musique. Not long after her first visit, Alphonsine had sent Gerfaut a money order to cover a month's salary. He had imme-diately gone and bought the radio, the pants, Gitane filters, and a plastic miniature chess set which was now on the bed-room floor with its pieces set up in the final position of a Vasyukov-Polugayewski match at the USSR championships of 1965 (White resigned after the thirty-second move).

"Georges!" said Alphonsine as she broke the seal on a bottle of Isle of Jura whisky. "What a horrible first name!"

"Everybody can't be called Alphonsine. Call me Ishmael. Call me cutie-pie, for all I care!"

"All right, that's fine. Cutie-pie. Perfect. I dumped him, you know, my boyfriend. When I got back to Paris. I wanted to come straight back here. I'm a real shit, aren't I?" As Gerfaut made no reply, she went on. "I wanted to, but I had commit-ments. And then, I wanted to think things over." She tittered. "No, seriously, I knew I was going to come back, but I wanted to do it slowly, elegantly. Why did you shave that sexy beard off? Do you know you look a bit like Robert Redford?"

"Ugh!" It was true, he did resemble Robert Redford. But, like a lot of men, he didn't much care for Robert Redford. "I was fed up with looking like—I don't know, like a bandit out of an Edmond About story. Commitments—what commitments? Are you in business? You seem pretty well-heeled."

Alphonsine pulled a stool up to the table and sat down. She poured whisky into two cracked cups, then put her elbows on the table, crossing her wrists and leaning her chin on them. She was wearing boots and suede pants. Her upper body was bare. She was not cold because a fire was roaring in the hearth. The hair at the nape of her neck was clammy with sweat. On the radio Johnny Guarnieri was superseded by a warm masculine voice retailing structuralist and leftist rubbish, then Dexter Gordon and Wardell Gray began to play.

"Wardell Gray—not this tenor, the other one," said Gerfaut, pointing uselessly at the receiver, "was found shot dead in a vacant lot. And Albert Ayler's body was fished out of the East River. It was Lee Morgan, his girlfriend, who bumped him off. Things like that exist! They really happen!"

"When I was nineteen," said Alphonsine absently, "I married a surgeon. He was crazily in love with me, the moron. It was only a civil marriage. We were divorced after five years, and I took him for every penny I could get. What do you mean, 'Things like that exist'? Don't say you're going to start again with your tales about killers!"

Gerfaut shook his head. He seemed preoccupied, indecisive. The laughter was almost completely gone from his features.

"The Isle of Jura," he said, turning to look at the bottle, "that's in the Hebrides. George Orwell had a small farm there. He wanted to get his life together, but he never really had the time before he died of tuberculosis."

"Well, you're a cheerful character, aren't you? A barrel of laughs. Who is this George Orwell, anyway?"

Gerfaut didn't reply. He knocked back his cup of Isle of Jura whisky in one.

"I'll have to make a decision one of these days," he remarked, but he didn't say what decision. "It'll wait. At least till this fog lifts. Let's go and make love, okay?"

They went and made love. The fog did not lift. For three days it did not lift. On the evening of the third day, the Peugeot

504 made its way slowly into the village with its fog lights on. It came to a halt in front of the church, across the street from the café-tabac.

Up at the Raguse house, Alphonsine and Gerfaut were at the table. Alphonsine was wearing a white terrycloth robe and thick American knop-wool socks. Gerfaut had on brown wide-wale corduroy pants and a plaid woolen shirt. Both he and Alphonsine smelled sweetly clean and well-soaped. They were eating bread and butter and drinking champagne. On the radio, a black woman sang about how, in the wee hours of the morning, when everyone is fast asleep, you lie awake in your bed and think of him, you can't help it. It was night, and the fog could be seen through the windows.

In the Peugeot 504, in front of the church, Carlo had switched on the overhead light to study his maps. He ticked off the name of the hamlet on a list. He had drawn up lists of all settlements of any size in the vicinity of the various points where Gerfaut might conceivably have fallen from a train. There was a host of possibilities, because the drifter had not been very clear. Carlo's list of most likely localities had forty-one entries. A second list, enumerating places where it was less likely but still very possible for Gerfaut to have ended up, comprised seventy-three names. There was even a third list. For forty-eight hours now, Carlo had been combing the mountains. The name of the hamlet where he now found himself occupied the twenty-third position on his first list.

The hit man put his lists and maps away, extinguished the interior light, and got out of the car. He crossed the muddy street and went into the café-tabac. Inside were three old men in tatty dark clothing and the owner, a fat man with suspenders. Carlo ordered coffee. He was brought a cup and saucer and a pot of coffee and coffee-stained sugar lumps in a plastic bowl meant to look like cut glass. Carlo asked for aspirin. And displayed his left index finger, which was bandaged up with gauze and adhesive tape.

"It's my finger. It hurts like hell."

"Piss on it!" exclaimed one of the old men. "Piss on it and don't wash it till sundown."

The hit man evinced a pale smile.

"I'd rather … I wonder … There wouldn't be a doctor hereabouts, would there?" (It was the twenty-third time he had asked the question in his two-day search.)

"Afraid not. You'll have to go back down." The owner scrutinized the hit man. "You have to go back, anyway—the road doesn't go any farther up the mountain."

"So," Carlo persisted, "if someone gets hurt or something, they go down into the valley? There's nobody at all who … I mean to say, there must be…."

"There used to be Corporal Raguse," put in the old fellow who had spoken earlier. "No more a corporal than I am, I might say. He's passed away, in any case."

Carlo stayed chatting for another quarter of an hour or so. He found out everything he wanted to know. He thanked the owner for the aspirin, paid for his coffee and for the round of rums he had bought, and walked out. For an instant, he stood motionless in the street. Through the thick fog he strove to make out lights, perhaps even lights at the Raguse house, which was no more than five hundred meters distant. But it was hopeless: he couldn't even see his 504 coupe four meters away.

Carlo was resolved now, in dealing with this moron Georges Gerfaut, to leave nothing to chance. The killer got back into his

JEAN-PATRICK MANCHETTE **105**

car and left the hamlet. Then, driving cautiously, his fog lights groping the whiteness, he descended slowly into the valley.

At Saint-Jean he found a hotel open and took a room for the night. Once settled in, he removed the dressing from his perfectly intact forefinger. He had carried the metal suitcase and the canvas bag upstairs himself. He placed both on the bed and began to lay out the things he proposed to wear the next day: cotton pants, checkered shirt, thick roll-neck sweater, boots. Then he carefully cleaned and oiled his weapons. And before going to bed he spent a long while studying his 1:25,000-scale maps. He had requested a wake-up call for five-thirty in the morning.

20

"I'm free!" cried Gerfaut. "I can make whatever I want of my existence. Believe me, I know what I'm talking about."

"You should go easy with that booze." Alphonsine's tone was not severe; she was smiling.

"I'm free!" Gerfaut added more liquor to his black coffee and drained the cup. "How would you like to come with me and kill something on the endangered-species list?" He leaped from the bed and clumsily pulled on his pants. He was in high spirits. "I don't love you, you know. You are very beautiful but a distinctly average person. I find you highly desirable."

"You're sloshed. Do you really want to go out?" Alphonsine pouted briefly. "Oh, well, perhaps it'll sober you up."

When the hit man saw the couple emerge from the house, a muscle twitched at his jaw line. Otherwise, the man was motionless, watching. As the crow flies, he was about seven hundred meters from the Raguse house and some two hundred and fifty meters higher up. He lay prone in a clump of low trees and continued to observe the house through his binoculars. The canvas bag was half-open beside him. Carlo had left the hotel at six, after settling up in cash. He had driven the length of a nearby valley as far as a pass, whence he had hiked six kilometers along narrow paths, reaching his present base of operations around seven-thirty. With him he had the automatic, its silencer, and the M6. The M6 was assembled, its back sight adjusted. Now he waited. It was twelve-fifteen. Gerfaut and the woman seemed to be laughing and jostling one another. Gerfaut had a gun slung over his shoulder. The hit man examined it through the powerful glasses. It looked like a respectable weapon—a Mauser-Bauer, perhaps, or a Weatherby. Or maybe an Omega III, like the one once presented to John Wayne—but, no, the breech was different.

The two were climbing straight toward the hit man. If they followed the path they were now on, they would soon veer left and then pass a little later less than three hundred meters from Carlo's position, putting themselves within perfect range. Should they not change direction and continue their ascent across pastureland, it was even possible that he would be able to pop them with the pistol, nice and quietly. The woman had to be killed, too, to prevent her from raising the alarm. Carlo had originally intended to wait until one or the other of them, or even both, left the house and then slip inside. As it was, things were working out even more simply. His victims were coming to him.

Three minutes later, following the path, Gerfaut and Alphonsine bore left. Very soon afterward, they were two hundred and sixty meters from the hit man and level with him. Alphonsine lost her footing slightly just ahead of Gerfaut and lurched to the right. Gerfaut put both his hands on her head and ran his fingers through her hair. As he did so, he laughed and rubbed his body against the young woman's, feeling her ass against him.

"You know," he said gaily, "I'm an idiot. A dumb cluck. What a crazy idea to go wandering around the mountains like this. I've had it up to here with these mountains. We are not weekenders, not—I don't know...."

Then the right side of Alphonsine's torso was ripped open. As though kicked by a horse, she was hurled sideways, and a glob of crushed bone, pulped flesh, fragments of bronchial tubes, atomized blood, and compressed air—along with the dumdum bullet driving this mass before it—broke explosively from her back. Gerfaut's hands were still outstretched before him, and he was astonished to find that Alphonsine's black hair was no longer between his fingers. The young woman's shoulder struck the ground just as Gerfaut heard the sound of the departing shot from over to his right. He dropped flat on his face, hearing the air split above him, and then a second report. At once stupefied and flooded by hate, his cheek plastered with earth, Gerfaut began unclipping his rifle from its sling. He turned toward Alphonsine, who was not moving. Her mouth was open, and her face was in the mud, and she was dead. The shock had stopped her heart instantly. Her companion's lips tightened at the sight of her open mouth and the terrible immobility of her features. A third bullet slammed into the earth behind Gerfaut's back, carving out a shallow cavity. Dirt and shards of stone lashed Gerfaut's back as the bullet, now completely flattened, ricocheted above him. He had freed the Weatherby now and, rolling over, he got it into firing position. In his sights something flashed briefly, and he pulled the trigger. His adversary stopped firing.

Gerfaut turned toward Alphonsine and looked at her again and kept looking at her until he understood fully that she was dead. Then he got to his feet. Slowly at first, then speeding up as he went, he ran toward the patch of shrubbery that he had aimed at. After a couple of minutes he made out the hit man rolling about in the bushes. Gerfaut's bullet had shattered the folding butt of the M6, spraying pieces of it in all directions; the bullet had then changed course, destroying the weapon before burying itself in Carlo's thigh and smashing his femur. The left side of Carlo's face was covered in blood: there, as in his side, myriad shards of plastic and light alloy were now embedded in the flesh. A clear-cut hole was visible in his pants at the left thigh, the fabric around it gummy with blood. The hit man brandished his Beretta in his right hand and fired at Gerfaut and missed, for he had lost his left eye and could no longer judge distances and was in shock.

It did not occur to Gerfaut to pull up and shoot the man dead. Instead, he went on running faster and faster, and the hit man went on firing at him and missed four more times before Gerfaut was upon him and delivering a great blow with his gun butt to his hand—whereupon the man dropped the automatic—and another to his head and another.

"You bastard!" Gerfaut cried. "You stinking dirty shit! Son of a bitch of a son of a bitch of a bastard!"

He stopped hitting Carlo and crouched down in front of him, his mouth open, his breath whistling in his throat, his chest heaving. He contemplated the hit man, who had slipped onto his side, the intact eye half-closed, and wondered, What shall I do? I'll do everything I'll torture him to death rip off his balls rip out his heart I must be calm but I am not all that agitated basically I am in fact ice-cold basically ice-cold.

He saw then that the man was dead. Gerfaut had smashed his skull with the gun butt. Shifting his weight from one buttock to the other, he drew closer to the hit man's body. He did indeed feel fairly calm and dispassionate. It was a little hard for him to concentrate, but he was not hesitant about what he had to do—this was not like all the other times over the last few months, ever since they had started trying to kill him; not hesitant, either, as he had been, when you came to think about it, for a very long time in his life as a manager and as a husband and as a father, and before that as a student and as a political militant and as a lover before his marriage and as an adolescent and even no doubt as a child.

He went through the dead man's pockets and found car keys and a driver's license in the name of Edmond Bron, born in Paris in 1944, domiciled in Paris on Avenue du Docteur Netter. Carlo had strictly nothing else on him.

Gerfaut left the corpse beneath the bushes along with the demolished M6 and the Weatherby. He picked up the Beretta automatic and put it in Carlo's canvas bag, which he took with him. He went back to where Alphonsine lay dead. Gerfaut's face was expressionless as he quickly searched the beautiful young woman without finding car keys or anything else of practical use. He got blood all over his hands. He left Alphonsine's body as it was and made his way back down to the house. He hurried; the exchange of gunfire had made a considerable din, though no one down in the village seemed yet to have paid it any mind.

Back at the house, he immediately spied Alphonsine's pocketbook. He took the keys and papers of the Ford Capri as well as what money there was—about a thousand francs. He gathered up such clothes as would pass in town and Carlo's canvas bag containing the Beretta. Then he got into the Capri, started it up, drove through the village, and proceeded from valley to valley, then from town to town, in the direction of Paris.

On the road, on the car radio, he picked up a number of things that would normally have appealed to him: Gary Burton, Stan Getz, Bill Evans. But they did nothing for him, and he turned the radio off. The fact was, it seemed to Gerfaut that it would be a long time before he would be able to enjoy music again.

21

It was getting late by the time he reached Auxerre and registered in a hotel as Georges Gaillard. He ate badly and slept
little. The radio news made no mention of him or of any killing
in the Alps. Gerfaut hoped he would be able to use the Capri
for a few more hours, and he was not to be disappointed, for
the next morning the car got him without incident to Paris.
Arriving at lunchtime, he abandoned the vehicle in Pantin,
leaving the doors unlocked and the key in the ignition, trust-
ing that, with a bit of luck, the thing would be stolen and any
pursuers thereby thrown off the scent. And stolen it was, by
what must have been well-organized felons, for no one ever
heard of the car again.

Gerfaut took the metro, changed at Gare de l'Est, and got
out at Opéra. It gave him great pleasure to be back in the city,
though he was not completely aware of it. He was carrying
Carlo's canvas bag with the Beretta and a few clothes in it. For a
few minutes, he enjoyed strolling through the maze of side
streets that lies to the east of Avenue de l'Opéra. Scurrying office workers, exhausted secretaries—a little world of grumbling
and irascible yet contented people flooded the snack bars and
cafés, rubbing shoulders with anxious currency dealers and
American students. Gerfaut bought *France-Soir* and leafed
through it abstractedly as he sat at the end of a counter eating
a frankfurter and fries. The usual things were going on in the
world, yet Gerfaut detected an evolution of some kind that was
hard to pin down. He finished his beer, left the copy of *France-
Soir* on the counter, and made his way to the headquarters of
the daily newspaper *Le Monde*. Across the boulevard, a staring
match was in progress between a large squad of uniformed po-

lice and a picket line barring the entrance to a bank. Gerfaut asked if he might consult back issues of the newspaper dating from almost a year earlier. He was told yes, certainly, and given directions; he set himself up, searched, and found what he was looking for. A male who had died at Troyes hospital the year before without regaining consciousness, after having been dropped off by an unidentified man, had turned out be a Monsieur Mouzon, a legal adviser by profession, from Paris, age forty-six. The cause of death was four bullet wounds inflicted by a 9mm weapon—no mention of any road accident. Gerfaut was not surprised.

Nine Mouzons were listed as residential subscribers in the Paris phone book, including someone described as a manufacturer of electric fans. In the listings by profession, however, Gerfaut found a consulting firm called Mouzon & Hodeng. He wrote down the number and as an afterthought noted the nine residential numbers, too. He walked across the post office and stood in line for a telephone cubicle. The business number elicited a recorded message informing him that the number was not currently in service. He began dialing the residential numbers one by one, leaving out the fan maker.

"Hello?"

A woman's voice.

Gerfaut pressed the button to make the connection.

"Monsieur Mouzon, please."

"Hold on, please. Who's calling?"

Gerfaut hung up. Tried another number. Same result. Tried a third. Busy signal. The fourth try was different.

"Hello?"

"Monsieur Mouzon, please."

"Monsieur Mouzon has died. Who is this?"

Gerfaut hung up, then remained motionless for a moment in the cubicle, thinking about death and about the horrible damage that bullets can do. Someone began tapping on the glass door with a set of keys in an obnoxious way. A fat man. Gerfaut came out.

"Fat idiot!" he said as he passed the man.

"What? What was that you said?"

But Gerfaut was already on his way out of the post office. He walked to Place de l'Opéra, studied a map of the metro, caught a train, changed at Invalides, and reemerged into the daylight at Pernety. It was only just four o'clock. Things were moving quickly. Having got his bearings, Gerfaut took Rue Raymond-Losserand, which was clogged with cars, delivery vans, road work, street vendors, and a good-humored and noisy throng. He found the house number he was looking for and went into the building where Mouzon had lived. There was no list of tenants. Gerfaut had no wish to ask the concierge. On the fifth floor he came upon an apartment door with a scrap of card pinned beneath the bell: MOUZON—GASSOWITZ, it said. Gerfaut rang. A man opened the door.

"Yes?"

The man wore beige cotton pants and a plaid lumberjack's shirt. He had greasy hair, thick lips, and a blue chin. With his Robert Mitchum build and beer belly to match, he didn't look particularly Polish—more like an ex–North African colonial type.

"I'm looking for Madame Mouzon."

"Yes?"

"That's it."

The man weighed the pros and cons, then seemed to reject

the idea of throwing Gerfaut down a flight of stairs to the next floor. He turned his head sideways, without taking his eyes off the visitor, and bellowed over his shoulder.

"Éliane!"

"What?"

"It's for you!"

Bustling could be heard within. The man redirected his chin toward Gerfaut and sighed softly, filling the four cubic meters of air on the landing with Ricard fumes. Éliane Mouzon arrived at the apartment door, but Gerfaut had to crane his neck to see her because the guy still blocked the way.

"What is it?"

She seemed tired, poor, and ordinary: not colorful at all, about forty-five, medium build, quite pretty despite very bad skin, lightly tinted hair, frankly lackluster black-and-white chiné suit, tan rayon blouse, torque of fake gold, bracelet ditto. She was artfully, almost beautifully made up. She was a slave to good taste, but she did not let herself go, and Gerfaut felt sympathy for her.

"I would like to speak to you in private," he told her. "About Monsieur Mouzon."

The skin around the woman's mouth blanched dramatically. She placed a palm against the hallway wall, and her eyelashes fluttered. The heavy-set guy glanced at her, then turned back to Gerfaut, lowering his head like a bull about to charge. His lips, too, were now ringed with white.

"Listen here, buddy," he growled, "I'm holding back because that's what she wants. But I don't know how long I can keep it up. So you'd better piss off, get it?"

"Stop it—he's not the one," said Mouzon's widow from behind his back.

"Oh, okay," said the heavyset guy—an irate Mr. Magoo struggling to focus and calm down at the same time. "I, er...."

"Come to think of it," broke in Gerfaut, "it's you I'd like to talk to. You—Monsieur Gassowitz, I take it? I have to talk to you. You have to let me in. Otherwise, I'll talk to the police, instead. I'm sure you wouldn't care for that, am I right?"

Gassowitz did not reply. He was thinking, and he appeared to be bothered by noise. But there was no noise. The landing was deathly quiet.

"I don't know who you are and I don't want to know," said the widow. "Leave me alone. Him, too."

Quite without warning, she burst into tears. Her cheap mascara ran into her eyes, and she wiped them with tiny fists, mumbling "Oh, my God" in an emotionless and exhausted voice.

"We can't just stand here on the landing," ruled Gerfaut.

Gassowitz retreated into the hallway, took the woman in his arms, and nestled her head to his shoulder. He stroked her hair. At the same time, he continued to stare at Gerfaut in a treacherous and angry way. Gerfaut proceeded gingerly into the apartment. Gassowitz used his foot to slam the door shut behind them.

"Baby," he murmured to the widow, "you go on into the bedroom."

Mouzon's widow disappeared into the bedroom. Gassowitz showed the visitor into a kitchen with a formica-topped table. His dark blue eyes were still shooting daggers at Gerfaut, who sat down without being invited. He noticed that he was sweating profusely and put it down solely to the emotional heat being generated on all sides in the small room.

"Shit!" he said. "I had absolutely no idea—I didn't anticipate anything like this. Listen, she's told you about it, hasn't she?

What I mean to say is, who was it that came the first time—that other time? A young man, dark, wasn't it? A young guy with wavy black hair and blue eyes? And a big toothy fellow, older?"

"It was the young one," said Gassowitz. "They both came together. But it was the young one who...."

"I killed him yesterday. I smashed his fucking skull; I busted his head in."

Words failing him, Gerfaut burst into tears. Folding his arms before him on the formica table, he laid his head on his forearms and sobbed strenuously. His tears stopped suddenly, but for several minutes he went on quaking and hyperventilating. He sounded like a Brazilian musical instrument.

Unsentimentally, Gassowitz tapped him on the shoulder.

"Here, you need a drink."

Gerfaut sat up, grasped the proffered mustard glass and tossed down the six centiliters of undiluted Ricard it contained. The pastis burned his throat. He felt it trickle ever so slowly, like a small raspy hot egg, down his tight gullet. Gassowitz sat down gently on a kitchen chair, his left leg extended and his right bent. Gerfaut glanced at the man's shoes—cheap tasseled things—and got the feeling that if at that moment he were to make a dash for the door, Gassowitz would plant his foot right in his face without bothering to get up from his chair.

"They killed Mouzon, obviously," said Gerfaut. "Then they came here to make sure that his widow knew nothing. If she had known anything, they would have finished her off, too. And they made doubly sure." He glanced at the white-lipped Gassowitz. "You are—what? Her lover, naturally. You met her after the fact. Listen, I don't want to know what they did to her."

"No, right," replied Gassowitz in an ordinary conversational tone.

"Listen," repeated Gerfaut, "I'm the guy that picked Mouzon up from the side of the road. It was me that dropped him off at the hospital. Then they caught up with me. It wasn't easy for them, but they caught up with me several times, and they did worse stuff to me than—well, I'm not sure that it was worse. I can try and give you the details if you like. I have to know if they were taking orders from someone. They saw me coming to Mouzon's rescue. They took my plate number. I suppose they figured I'd heard his last words. It's all so banal, it's pathetic. I can't...."

"I want the details."

"Okay, I'll try." And Gerfaut told his whole story to the heavyset guy. It took more than half an hour, because Gassowitz kept asking questions, to some of which Gerfaut had no answer. Gassowitz wanted to know why Gerfaut had not gone to the police, and Gerfaut said that that would have been a pain in the ass.

"But still, I mean, going right ahead like that!"

"Yes, yes, I know. But I can't explain. I can't really understand it myself."

"Maybe you were just sick of everything?"

"But could it be that simple?"

"It could."

Gassowitz also wanted to know how come the two thugs had found Gerfaut at the gas station, the time the toothy man had gone up in flames, but Gerfaut couldn't explain that, either.

Éliane Mouzon came in to see what was going on, her pretty face collapsed and ravaged. Gassowitz sent her back into the bedroom, promising to explain everything later, but he did so with great tenderness.

"That's it," said Gerfaut at last. "Is that what you wanted to know?"

"I suppose so," grumbled Gassowitz.

Gerfaut drank a little Ricard diluted with water.

"I don't know why I told you all this. The only thing I'm interested in is finding whoever gave those two bastards their orders. And you know nothing. Your—Madame Mouzon knows nothing, either; otherwise, they wouldn't have let her off that easily, and...."

"I'm interested in that, too," Gassowitz broke in.

"Okay, but you don't know anything, you don't know why...."

"Hodeng."

"Huh?"

"Philippe Hodeng. Mouzon and he were partners. They were legal advisers. You know, they got pathetic people to pay their debts by throwing a scare into them. With letterheads and legal-sounding threats, that sort of thing."

"Debt recovery?"

"Something like that. But sleazy. And they came across all kinds of stuff. They would get information on people, then offer their so-called services. Mouzon was an ex-cop—I expect you knew that?"

"No, I didn't."

"Well, he was. He was canned or whatever you call it. Something about theft—while he was still in the police, I mean. But he was amnestied later—which is how he was able to set up his consulting business. Hodeng, I don't know exactly, but I think he was a sort of stool pigeon of Mouzon's when he was still a cop. Then, later, they went into partnership, get it?"

"I get it, all right."

"And just after Mouzon died, the next day, Hodeng met with a serious accident."

"Is he dead?"

"No."

"Can he be found?"

"Monsieur Gerfaut, I am going to take you to him. I want to go with you. Give me a moment—I need a word with Éliane, so she doesn't worry. But I want to go with you. I can because I've been out of work recently. And I have to, you see—I simply must go with you."

"Fine," said Gerfaut. "Fine, yes. Good."

22

They found Philippe Hodeng where he was at that point in his life: in a filthy retirement home in Chelles; and in the shape that he was in at that point in his life: helpless and almost mute. He occupied a dingy dark room on the second floor of one of the four or five buildings that made up the institution. In the courtyard, sycamores laden with young leaves of garish green hung over an admixture of gravel and dog turds. Philippe Hodeng was fifty-two, but he might have been seventy or a hundred, for that matter. He sat in a wheelchair with a tartan blanket over his paralyzed legs. In falling out of the window at Mouzon & Hodeng's offices, he had fractured his spine. At some point, he had suffered brutal trauma to the throat. His larynx had been crushed. He had undergone a tracheotomy and various other operations. He was now a cripple, and his vocal cords were destroyed. Although voice-retraining techniques existed that could have helped him, Hodeng could not afford such treatment. But, by following the instructions given in an American book, he was beginning to produce organized sounds once more by subtly contracting his diaphragm and trachea. The result, a raucous, piping, and pneumatic register, was somehow simultaneously reminiscent of François Mauriac and Roland Kirk.

Hodeng was dressed in a shiny, slim-fitting suit, a ratty nylon shirt with a gaping collar, and a Basque beret. His toothless mouth was surrounded by a multitude of white wrinkles and crevices. His glasses were green, and his hair was a yellowish white. To put it in a nutshell, his condition was desperate.

Gerfaut and Gassowitz had no difficulty finding him. They presented themselves at the reception desk, where a fat girl with unkempt hair, flabby cheeks, and rolls of flesh under her arms gave them directions without hesitation and without curiosity. The fact was that the old people in the place were left much to their own devices: the rooms were cleaned now and then, the bedding changed every couple of weeks, meals served in a refectory for those who were mobile and brought up to those who were not, and anyone who wet their bed got a chewing out. That was it.

The problems began after Gerfaut and Gassowitz entered Hodeng's room, when the patient, reaching beneath the bedclothes, produced a small 7.65mm automatic, with the word VENUS inscribed in large letters on the grip, and pointed it at the visitors.

"Hey!" said Gassowitz. "Take it easy. We're from Social Security."

As he spoke, the massive Gassowitz seized an empty umbrella stand and whirled it in an arc; it caught the little automatic and wrenched it from Hodeng's fingers and sent it skittering across the dirty carpet. Gassowitz took a step forward and nudged the weapon under the bed with the tip of his shoe. Hodeng put his wheelchair violently into reverse, whining, whistling, and grunting, and ended up backed against the wall. That was when Gerfaut and Gassowitz explained the nature of their business with him—or at least the parts Hodeng needed to know. And Hodeng supplied the information requested.

It went pretty quickly and simply.

"No! Afraid," the invalid wheezed at one stage in the conversation. It sounded more like "Oo! Ray," but by this time Gerfaut and Gassowitz could fairly easily understand the sounds he produced.

"They can't do anything else to you," said Gerfaut.

"One ... ah ... ivv."

Gassowitz interpreted: "He says he wants to go on living."

"Listen, Hodeng," said Gerfaut, "I can understand that. That's why I've told you some of what they did to me. It's also why you can take it from me that either you talk or I'll kill you. Tell me who's behind those two bastards or I'll kill you. Here and now. Get it? You don't believe I'll do it?"

After a very short moment's reflection Hodeng nodded vigorously and asked for paper and pencil. He then covered four pages of a datebook with tiny handwriting. From time to time Gerfaut or Gassowitz interrupted him with requests for clarification. At last he had finished, and there were no further questions. Gerfaut stuffed the datebook pages in his pocket.

"We'll try and make sure this doesn't drop you back in the shit."

"Ssss ... too ... wid, huh?" said Hodeng with great difficulty. "Unning to live!" He indicated his useless legs, his useless throat, then the shitty room, and the shitty landscape outside; as his gestures tailed off, he smiled self-deprecatingly. "Kill him," he whirred. "Kill at bastard, kay?"

Gerfaut and his out-of-work companion headed toward Paris in Gassowitz's clapped-out Peugeot 203, then bypassed the city via the ring road. It took them a long time, for it was rush hour and the ring road was backed up. They weren't talking; they were barely thinking. About six-forty-five, they took the superhighway to the west. Once past the Chartres turnoff they were able to drive fast. Gerfaut opened the canvas bag lying at his feet on the car floor. He took out the Beretta and silencer. He handled the weapon for a few moments to make sure he understood its operation. The 203 left the highway at Meulan. Gassowitz stopped in front of a pharmacy that was still open, got out of the car, and went in. He emerged with two pairs of rubber gloves of the kind used by housewives for washing dishes. He gave one pair to Gerfaut. Each man thrust his pair of gloves into a jacket pocket. The 203 set off again and took the road to Magny-en-Vexin.

"It's one thing for you," said Gerfaut. "I imagine you love Éliane Mouzon. As for me, though, the woman who was killed up there in the mountains, I didn't love her, you know. She was really very beautiful, but...." He broke off and fell silent for a good minute. "Perhaps I shouldn't be as angry as I am."

"Do you want to stop for dinner and think things over?"

"No."

"How about I drop you at a train station and you leave me your gun?"

"No, absolutely not," was Gerfaut's reply.

They passed through Magny-en-Vexin and followed the sign for the hamlet of Vilneuil. Still ten kilometers away, Gassowitz pulled over and parked on the roadside. Without speaking, the two men sat in the car and waited for night.

23

After dining on canned food and fruit in the kitchen, Alonso put the dirty dishes in the dishwasher, which already held those left from breakfast. The Sharp stereo system was playing Chopin. Elizabeth trotted in her master's footsteps as he toured the house checking that the windows were properly locked. At each window he paused to look out through his binoculars. He had his Colt officer's target pistol at his belt, in a holster with a flap. Alonso was dressed in well-worn khaki shorts and shirt. White chest hairs poked through the front of his shirt. He moved carefully throughout the house and was sure to inspect every single opening to the outside. The year before, two so-called private detectives had come upon him quite by chance, while hunting in the vicinity of Magny-en-Vexin for an important American criminal. And they had tried to get Alonso to talk. His response—as a matter of routine, so to speak—was to sic his contract killers on them. (It was not the first time he had drawn on the skills of Carlo and Bastien to preserve his incognito status: he had had them kill four people liable to lead his enemies to him.) And Bastien and Carlo had indeed taken care of things—except for the matter of Gerfaut, which remained for Alonso an annoying and disquieting mystery. He had insisted that the imbecile who had taken Mouzon to the hospital be taken out. Later, he had learned from the radio that Gerfaut and Carlo had disappeared and that Bastien was dead. Or perhaps it was Carlo that was dead and Bastien and Gerfaut that had vanished: he did not really know which of his hit men had perished in the flames at the gas station. Now, eleven months later, his hope was that they were all dead—the two hit men and the imbecile, too. At all events, he had never heard another thing about them.

Alonso sat down at the desk in his study. The bullmastiff lay down on the carpet nearby. He uncapped his Parker fountain pen and spent an hour working on his memoirs. *An end must be put to violence,* he wrote. *The best way to end violence is to punish those who resort to it, whatever their position in society. Generally speaking, such individuals are not very numerous. And that is why, in principle, representative democracy has always seemed to me the best way to run a nation. Sadly, the countries of the free world are prevented from living according to their principles, because communist subversion insinuates itself into their organism and brings on recurrent and endemic attacks of decay.* Alonso got up and made yet another round of the house, and closed all the shutters. Night was falling. It was a quarter after eight. The Sharp system carried Grieg to every room, then it changed the record and carried Liszt. Alonso went upstairs with a bulky volume of Clausewitz. He drew himself a very hot bath, undressed, and slipped into the water with a grimace. He had placed the Colt on the lid of the toilet alongside the bathtub. He settled into the water with little sighs of either discomfort or pleasure. At ten-twenty-two the extremely loud Lynx alarm installed in the attic was set off, Gerfaut and Gassowitz having just then forced the barred entrance to the property.

Stricken, Alonso dropped *On War* between his legs into the hot water. He bounded from the bathtub in a great spray of water and grabbed his gun. The weapon slipped from his fingers and fell to the floor. Alonso dropped on all fours to retrieve it. In the overgrown garden in front of the residence, Gerfaut and Gassowitz halted for a moment at the wail of the alarm, which must have been audible for kilometers around. Alonso's house was about one hundred meters from its nearest neighbors in the hamlet. Gerfaut groaned, then raced on. In his left hand was the Beretta, and in his right, one of the tire irons the two men had used to pry open the iron entrance gate. Gassowitz hesitated a moment longer, then chased after Gerfaut. He held the other tire iron and a square Wonder flashlight that was turned off. It was not yet pitch black—you could still just see where you were going. Gerfaut had reached the front of the house and was already going to work on a shutter with his tire iron.

In the upstairs bathroom Alonso got back to his feet, Colt in hand. His eyes were bulging, and he was having difficulty breathing. His pallid, pudgy body streamed with bathwater. He made a series of staccato and incomplete movements suggesting he meant to dash toward the door or at least dash somewhere. Mechanically, he rescued his book from the bottom of the bath, scowling in irritation; he shook water from it, then pivoted in search of somewhere to put it down. Through the wild racket of the incessantly bleating alarm, Alonso heard Elizabeth's furious barking down on the ground floor; he also heard wood and glass shattering.

Gerfaut had ripped open the window shutters of the study, heaved himself up onto the window ledge without the slightest precaution and driven his heel through the glass. The lights were on in the room. Gerfaut climbed through the window and ended up on the writing desk. Snarling, the bullmastiff leaped for his throat. Gerfaut discharged the Beretta into the animal's maw. The dog was catapulted sideways into a wall, splattering it with blood. She slid along the floor, regrouped, and returned to the attack, growling horribly. Part of her lower jaw was missing, and what was left of it was all broken and twisted, yet she sprang onto the writing desk and tried to bite the intruder. Meanwhile, Gassowitz in his turn had hoisted himself onto the windowsill. Gerfaut fired three times into the dog's body, then kicked her to the floor. Elizabeth fetched up once more against the wall, still alive, thrashing about and trying to get back up. Gerfaut began to vomit. He clambered from the desk, scattering the onionskin that Alonso used for writing his memoirs. He rushed at the dog, thrust the barrel of the Beretta against her skull and frenziedly pulled the trigger. He quickly emptied the weapon. The bullmastiff bitch was dead. Still retching, Gerfaut tore the magazine from the automatic, took another clip from his jacket pocket, reloaded, and recocked the gun.

"Oh, boy!" exclaimed Gassowitz as he contemplated the carnage.

Then Alonso burst into the study, naked, plump, and dripping wet, with a gun in one hand and a large sodden book in the other. He raised his weapon, but Gerfaut was faster and he put a bullet in Alonso's belly. The naked man fell into a sitting position with his back against the frame of the communicating door. He let go of his gun and his book and, grimacing with pain, brought both hands to the place where the projectile had entered his body.

"I am Georges Gerfaut," said Georges Gerfaut. "And you are Alonso Eduardo Rhadamès Philip Emerich y Emerich, am I right?"

"No, I am not! I'm not him!" said Alonso. "Oh! Oh! This hurts!"

"It's him, all right," said Gassowitz.

"What did you say?" asked Gerfaut, who could not hear Gassowitz on account of the still-wailing alarm, not to mention the Liszt.

"Yes!" screamed Alonso. "Yes! It is me! I'll wipe you out! I'll find you! I shit on you!"

The effort of shouting exhausted Alonso. He leaned his head against the door frame and began to moan softly. Gerfaut raised the Beretta. Gassowitz grabbed his arm.

"Let him suffer."

Gerfaut lowered the gun. Blood was pouring from the naked man's stomach.

"No, that's intolerable," said Gerfaut. And he brought the Beretta back up, advanced two steps, and killed Alonso instantly with a shot to the head.

Gassowitz and Gerfaut looked at one another. Then they remembered that the alarm was still howling and that this was no time to dawdle. One after the other, they clambered in turn onto the writing desk and thence onto the window ledge, before jumping back down into the wild garden. They ran, tripping over tufts of grass and bushes, until they got to the gateway. On the road outside were three men with flashlights, country people from the hamlet wearing work overalls and berets or caps.

"What's going on?" they demanded of Gerfaut and Gassowitz as the two emerged from the property.

Gerfaut and Gassowitz pushed past the men and took off running down the road.

"Stop! Thief!" shouted the locals.

Gerfaut and Gassowitz reached the dirt road at whose entrance they had parked the old 203. They got into the car panting, hearts thumping. The locals did not give chase; they conferenced in the road and agreed that they ought to go and see what was happening at Mister Taylor's and then later, if need be, alert the police. The 203 reversed out of the dirt road about a hundred meters from the locals, turned and drove away from them, and vanished round a bend.

"That was disgusting," said Gerfaut.

"No," answered Gassowitz. "It made me feel better. Because Éliane has been avenged, you know what I mean?"

"Yes, you think so?" Gerfaut's tone was positive now.

Later, as they headed down the highway toward Paris, Gerfaut asked Gassowitz if he would drop him off at Place d'Italie when they got to the city. Which is what Gassowitz did, just after ten-fifteen that night. The two men shook hands. The 203 disappeared. Gerfaut was a stone's throw from home, meaning from his permanent address. He walked over, took the elevator up to his floor, and rang his own doorbell. Béa opened the door to him. She opened her mouth wide and her eyes wide, and she looked at him and covered her mouth with her hand in stupefaction.

"I'm back," said Gerfaut.

24

After Béa had asked him, tonelessly, to come in, Gerfaut went through to the living room, which had not changed. His expression was intense, preoccupied. He automatically turned on the quadraphonic system and played a record; his choice was a duet by Lee Konitz and Warne Marsh. Then he went and sat on the couch. Béa stood in the doorway of the room, looking at him. Abruptly, she turned and went into the kitchen. There she leaned for a moment against the wall. Her jaw worked as though she were speaking, but she did not speak. Finally, she came out with a glass of Cutty Sark with plenty of ice and water for Gerfaut and a glass of Cutty Sark straight up for herself. Gerfaut said thank you. He was leafing through some papers on the coffee table. Among them was a six-month-old letter from his chess partner, the retired math teacher in Bordeaux, in which the latter explained to Gerfaut, in a measured way that barely concealed his underlying irritation, that he had no choice but to consider Gerfaut the loser by default in view of his failure to reply within a reasonable time to Black's seventh move (7... Dc7). Gerfaut looked up.

"What did you say?"

"I said, where did you come from?" said Béa in a hollow voice.

"I don't know."

"You smell of vomit. There's vomit on your pants. You're filthy." She sobbed, then rushed to Gerfaut on the couch, encircling him in her arms and pressing her body tightly against his. "Oh, my darling, my darling, my sweetheart, where have you been?"

"But it's true. I don't know."

And that has been his story ever since. He claims that he doesn't know. Though he was not the first person to use the word amnesia in his case, he now readily speaks of his memory loss when the subject comes up. According to him, he remembers nothing of his own experience between the moment on a July evening when he left his vacation house in Saint-Georges-de-Didonne to buy cigarettes and the moment on a May evening when he found himself wandering not far from his home in Paris with vomit on his pants. His account, be it said, is lent a measure of credibility by a scar on his scalp which is consistent with a gunshot wound, or a blow from a blunt instrument, that might well have administered a severe shock to the brain.

Gerfaut was interrogated several times by the police and by an examining magistrate. A judicial investigation was in fact opened into the deaths of Bastien and, particularly, of the young gas-station attendant. Gerfaut conceded the possibility of his having rented the Taunus, along with the possibility that his amnesia may have been brought on by a shock received during the mayhem at the service station. Which would mean that his memory loss was retroactive; but such a thing is not rare in the annals of medicine—far from it. Similarly, in the event of Liétard's testifying, Gerfaut had intended to assert that he had no recollection of having visited him, nor of the content of any conversation with him, nor of any mind-boggling tale about hired killers. That was never required, however, since Liétard—who reads no newspapers and barely ever listens to the radio and is interested only in the movies—never testified, indeed did not know that Gerfaut had mysteriously disappeared from July to May, and knows nothing of it to this day.

The crippled Philippe Hodeng died in August. The country

people who had witnessed the flight of the murderers of Alonso Emerich y Emerich were able to supply only a vague and useless description. No link could therefore be established between the killing of Alonso and Georges Gerfaut, and indeed no one even thought of it, any more than they thought of associating Gerfaut with the murders of Alphonsine Raguse-Peyronnet and an unidentified male carrying a false driver's license in the name of Edmond Bron. For that double murder, committed in La Vanoise at the beginning of May, the only suspect is a certain Georges Sorel. The one person who could tell a great deal about Georges Gerfaut and what he was doing between July and May is Gassowitz, but Gassowitz has every reason in the world to lay low.

Gerfaut's position is thus unassailable, and he knows it. As a leftist militant in his distant youth, he read manuals and personal narratives on keeping inquisitive policemen and investigating judges at bay. And he has indeed kept all such at bay, never wavering from his claim of total ignorance and always presenting himself as candid, cooperative, and agonized. Investigators have wearied of asking him questions, and interviews, after growing rare, have now ceased.

As for his professional life, he has succeeded, despite the economic crisis, in finding a management-level job at his old company. He has taken a cut in salary, and his responsibilities are fewer, but since he is a model employee, there is no doubt that after a probationary period his position and remuneration will be comparable to what they were before his disappearance.

During those ten months of Gerfaut's absence, Béa remained faithful. After his reappearance she babied him a good deal for a time, then resumed her usual healthily detached attitude. Sexually speaking, everything is copacetic between Béa and her husband, except when Gerfaut drinks too much and takes ages to reach orgasm. Gerfaut drinks bourbon now in preference to scotch. This is the only way in which his tastes have altered, but the switch came in September, so it doesn't appear to be linked to his disappearance. In August, the Gerfauts spent their vacation in Saint-Georges-de-Didonne, in a rented house that turned out almost by chance to be attractive and comfortable, so that Gerfaut was delighted with their stay. For a while, Béa urged Gerfaut to undergo psychoanalysis to try and discover what his mind was concealing, but she was met with an obstinate refusal and eventually gave up, and now never mentions it.

For Gerfaut, in short, things are hunky-dory. All the same, there are evenings when he drinks far too much Four Roses bourbon and then takes barbiturates, which instead of getting him to sleep plunge him into a state of ruminative agitation and melancholy. Tonight is a case in point. After making love, not very satisfactorily, with Béa, he lay awake as she fell asleep, then sat in the living room listening to Lennie Niehaus and Brew Moore and Hampton Hawes and drinking more Four Roses. In his journal he reflected that he could have been an artist or, better, a man of action, an adventurer, a Foreign Legionnaire, a conquistador, a revolutionary, the list goes on. Then he put his shoes and jacket back on and took the elevator down to the basement parking garage. He got into the Mercedes, which needed a serious overhaul after spending ten months garaged in Saint-Georges-de-Didonne, but which now runs fine. Gerfaut entered the outer ring road at the Porte d'Ivry. It is now two-thirty or maybe three-fifteen in the morning, and Gerfaut is circumnavigating Paris at 145 kilometers per hour and listening to West Coast musicians, chiefly blues, on his tape deck.

There is no way of saying exactly how things will turn out for Georges Gerfaut. In a general way, you can see how things will work out for him, but not in detail. In a general way, the relations of production that contain the reason why Georges is racing along the ring road with diminished reflexes, playing the particular music he is playing, will be destroyed. Perhaps Georges will then show something other than the patience and servility that he has always shown up to now. It is not likely. Once, in a dubious context, he lived through an exciting and bloody adventure; after which, all he could think of to do was to return to the fold. And now, in the fold, he waits. If at this moment, without leaving the fold, Georges is racing around Paris at 145 kilometers per hour, this proves nothing beyond the fact that Georges is of his time. And of his space.

Jean-Patrick Manchette (1942–1995) rescued the French crime novel from the grip of stodgy police procedurals—restoring the noir edge by virtue of his post-1968 leftism. Today, Manchette is a totem to the generation of French mystery writers who came in his wake. Jazz saxophonist, political activist, and screen writer, Manchette was influenced as much by Guy Debord as by Dashiell Hammett.

Printed in the USA
CPSIA information can be obtained
at www.ICGtesting.com
JSHW082214140824
68134JS00014B/617

9 780872 863958